Covered Wagon Odyssey

The Story of Andrew and Mary Knapp

STEVEN LEE

PublishAmerica
Baltimore

PublishAmerica has allowed this work to remain exactly as the author intended, verbatim, without editorial input.

Hardcover 978-1-4489-3717-2
Softcover 978-1-4489-7632-4
PUBLISHED BY PUBLISHAMERICA, LLLP
www.publishamerica.com
Baltimore

Printed in the United States of America

This book is dedicated to the memory of my great-grandparents, Roy and Goldie Knapp, whose influence on this work—and on my life—could never be overestimated.

Acknowledgements

The following people, in alphabetical order, have contributed to this book in various ways, including their computer skills, information sharing, proofreading, pictures, interest, and general support: Brittany Butcher, Mildred Fehrenbacher, Adrienne Golubski, Bill Knapp, Jane Knapp, Bernetta Mason, Carole Ann Musgrave, Joan Potter, Roxy Potter, Doug Slagley, John Upton, Barbara Walker, and Linda Windland.

CHAPTER 1
Uprooting

April 15, 1890. Falls, Kansas. A mild temperature had combined with air saturated with humidity and pollen to create a heavy air that sluggishly blew in the west windows of the frame house on the edge of town, set back from the road several hundred feet, surrounded by maples that pushed forth their wing-like seeds into the atmosphere of spring's optimism. Mary Knapp stood at this west window with its curtains that seemed to almost be breathing asthmatically in and out, in and out. Surveying this, the best parlor, she took in, as her eyes followed the contour of the room, a precious space that once danced with laughter of her children, husband, in-laws, neighbors, and herself—but now it was forlorn and silent. Vacancy was all she took in, except for the overstuffed divan. It would not fit in the wagon; it must stay behind.

Every flourish she had bestowed on this room now raced before her in a confused list: the woodwork painted white, the wallpaper living with peacocks and mimosa trees, the china ceiling fixture encircled with shimmering pink glass beads, the doorway where her three children's heights were recorded in pencil. Today she must leave all of this comfort and familiarity forever. In ten minutes her feet must take her unwillingly to a covered wagon stuffed with eight years of married life. To Mary, who clung to the known and found stability in it, the pain overwhelmed her, her lips and chin quivering as she struggled to regain composure.

"I can't, I won't let Andrew and the children see me like this. I'm strong. I've pulled up roots many times in my life and recovered. I'm certainly able to bear this gamble, this pig in a poke," she tried to convince herself. Despite this internal supportive talk, a sudden wave of sadness and loss disabled her spirit. Sobbing in her hands cupped to her face, her whole frame shook with emotion, greatly unsteadying her firm resolve to be Spartan and silent, no matter what.

As she swayed backward, the windowsill sliced into the small of her back, and the strain of her slight weight on the curtain, caught between her back and the open window, caused a ripping of several coarse strands of thread that artistically hemmed the curtains in curves and elipses.

As if forgetting today's evacuation plan, she whirled around at the tearing sound, thinking she must put this injury right, must get her sewing basket which contained the caramel-colored thread. Then the thought struck her: no urgency to repair this mishap existed. New owners would probably replace these curtains, anyway. And the house in Illinois was, today, only an abstract dream that didn't have any windows that needed curtains.

Not realizing that the front door had opened and closed with its customary groan of the long-corroded spring, Mary said, into the empty room, "I don't want to do this. I don't—." A small, thin, knowing voice overlapped her sentence as she finished it with, "But you said, Ma—."

"Roy, why are you in here? Your place is looking after your sister in the wagon," Mary admonished him. Born two years ago, sister Mabel was active and prone to wander off, seeking her own amusement, unafraid of unfamiliar people, places, and animals. And it was the animals, the horses hitched to the wagon, that Mary was most concerned about. She had expressly assigned Roy to watch after her and to keep her close to the wagon, in order to avoid a later delay in departure in search of her.

As Roy looked up at her with those penetrating blue eyes of his, Mary felt unarmed and caught in a flagrantly illegal act. Up until today, she had maintained an iron shell of control and optimism. For him to see her like this made her theatrical performance of the last six months seem to evaporate like a vapor in front of her eyes—and his. She had lost all energy and loyalty needed to play her character in the drama.

This second son, Roy, not yet five, had an almost maddening intuition; he seemed to read her mind, in particular when she wanted her mind to be hidden from him the most. Knowing Roy's alertness, it was pointless to try to fool him: she knew there was no use whatsoever to attempt to explain away her tears by saying a speck of dirt had lodged in her eye or that a sneeze was imminent. Roy had heard her words, knew their import, and she knew exactly what he would say next, for he was not finished quoting her incessantly repeated words from the last months: "We're all going to be happy in our new home in Illinois." Though she had drilled these words into her children, they had not taken root in her own heart as the absolute truth. Now that she faced the extinction of her life here, she fundamentally could not convince her heart that such happiness in Illinois would ever be. Her heart had an ache as big as the room she was surveying.

Desperately, she did not want to leave, but she also did not want to admit this to her children. As an adult, rational parent, she had painted a rosy panoramic picture of their new, exciting, pioneering life to make the move seem like a blessed exodus.

STEVEN LEE

Yet, all the while her psyche shouted a loud, obstinate NO. So, she had lived a duplicity, encouraging her kids to look happily forward to the migration while, in her soul and in her ever present anxiety, she dreaded the leaving day.

And now that day was here. The mud roads were beginning to somewhat dry up, the move needed to be concluded before planting time, the cold was behind, and the hot was yet to come.

April 15, 1890. The perfect day to begin a new life. Nevertheless, this was the saddest day of her life.

"But you said, Mom, that we're all going to be happy in our new home in Illinois," Roy reminded her from that mind that never missed any detail of life but closed on it like a bear trap.

Innocently, pleadingly, Roy asked, "So, why are you crying?"

Letting loose of the frayed fabric she was unconsciously rolling between thumb and forefinger, Mary slid down the wall to the floor in a characteristic action that immediately brought Roy into her lap. Holding him to her, her hands combing through his thick brown hair, gravity continued to pull at the tears; they jumped off her swollen cheeks like the swimmers she'd seen leaping from the rocks into the namesake falls of the community.

"We don't always get what we want, Roy. It may be hard for you to understand this, but sometimes we must give in to what's best for others, even when it hurts," Mary spoke softly, her lips touching his hair.

"Today we are starting a new life, but letting go of the old life is tearing me apart inside," she shuddered and winced. An invisible hand encircled her throat, and stabbing pain matched emotion. Raising her head and pulling for air, she once again gave way to tears.

10

"However, Roy, I promise you this: today is the last time I will cry about leaving, and no matter where we live or what happens to us in the future, I will always love you."

With those words, a heavy door slammed shut in her mind, with a darkness that consciousness could not penetrate.

"Enough," Mary whispered to herself in a fatalistic tone.

Standing up, Roy in front of her skirt that hit the floor, she dared not take a final reminiscent stroll about the room with her eyes that leaked sentimentality. Instead, she fastened her attention in a straight line from herself through the front door that framed the waiting wagon and team on the other side of the picket fence. She must not lose sight of the wagon, her passage to Canaan, or she would drown in the Red Sea.

On the other side of the wagon, Andrew Knapp and his brother Burdett, known colloquially as Burd, were lazily leaning on the wagon bed chewing the stems of grass already gone to seed. They stared at a blank sky and felt awkward in conversation for the first time in their lives. Always inseparable, only three years apart in age, the brothers had shared every major life event: such as when Andrew had crushed his leg in a logging accident, two monstrous oak logs rolling together and pinning him like a wringer until Burd and others spotted him and pried the rollers apart; or like when Burdett lost his footing and fell head first into the falls of Judas Creek but was plucked from the rocks to safety by Andrew and their father, Alexander; or when Andrew announced he would be leaving home and starting a married life with Mary, Burd standing behind the smokehouse door crying.

To live apart was like separating an egg's yolk from its white, a risky, unnatural thing to attempt. Silent contemplation could not give way to words in the two men; language would smack of weakness and lack of confidence. So, the two brothers stood with their hearts brimming with words never spoken. They were destined to say goodbye just as it they'd see each other tomorrow at the Purification Methodist Church and sing "Will the Circle Be Unbroken?" even though their next conversation could be years or decades away, or never.Andrew, combing through his many thoughts of the moment, focused on the impulsive trade he had made during the train ride: the patent on his steam iron swapped for 120 acres of farm ground in southern Illinois.

Suddenly through nearby weeds and brush, two children burst into view, relieving the brothers of the awkwardness they wanted escape from. Their attention turned to little Mabel, who, laughing with impish delight, raced to her dad and hid in his coattails. In hot pursuit, Charlie, red-faced, was clearly furious with her.

"Dad, she took off through the pasture, and I've been chasing her in circles ever so long. Roy wasn't watching her as Mom told him to, so I took his place. Are you going to punish her?" Charlie gasped.

"Punish her for being a happy, high-spirited young lady that no harm has come to? I don't think so," Andrew laughed. "But, Mabel, don't take off again. We're ready to leave now."

Half hidden beside her father, Mabel twisted on one foot and then the other, stuck her fingers in her mouth, and wiped her nose on her calico sleeve. She was safe from harm with her dad. Her wide open eyes looked up at him as he gazed into the distance. Incapable of long-term, long-distance thinking, Mabel was only aware that she loved to frustrate her brothers and that her dad was her protector against them.

Through the front gate, Mary and Roy joined the others. All three children climbed into the wagon bed with its canvas covering supported by hoops, husband and wife took their places on the seat, a switch goaded the horses, and the wagon started east. The sun, now straight above them, beamed down on the home, and Mary turned just once as the wagon crested a small hill a mile away to take a mental picture. Seeing her glance backward, Andrew gave the reins a quick snap, urging the team to quicken its pace.

April 15, 1890: Left Falls, Kansas this morning for our home in Illinois in our covered wagon. Crossed Lions Creek and stopped there for dinner. Then drove to 2 miles East of Skiddy and stopped there for the night. The wind was in the East all day. Commenced raining just as supper was ready.

CHAPTER 2
A Risk

Green. The color green. It totally surrounded him and submerged him. He was standing in a dense underbrush of blackberry briars, wild grape vines, saplings of sassafras, sumac bushes, and grasses so green. Even though little light reached him, he could sense the color of lush, green life all around him. He wondered, could Mrs. McMullen, our photographer, capture such a vibrant image as this? Could the deliciousness of this moment so full of life be transferred to paper permanently to savor when sorely needed in the future?

No, this won't last, so I must catch the image in my mind, he told himself.

Now, looking beyond himself in this thicket, he, for the first time, could make out trees in the semi-darkness. He examined a sycamore a few feet in front of him, following its papery bark down to its roots stretching fingerlike into the ground and then up to the first lateral branches, massive, up, up to the top-most visible branches that meshed with other trees, nearly shutting out the sun straight overhead, a few pinpoints of light piercing the intense green ceiling.

Turning to the left he sensed another tree, and behind him was the scaly bark of another. Yes, alone in this unreal world, he inhaled and drank in the life all around him. This is what he had imagined it would be like.

Suddenly a gust of wind penetrated the tightly packed woods; leaves snapped and whipped, squirrels recovered their precarious footholds in the trees, ancient oaks groaned at the disturbance but, then, sighing, returned to their resting state.

Andrew felt joy the he had found such a supremacy in nature.

Closing his eyes, he smiled.

In this moment of perfect peace, there was a pull on his pant leg.

The pull was repeated with the words, "Pa, wake up. Come on!"

It was Mabel, sitting in the dirt by the wagon, and he was on his side with this right cheek almost touching the wheel spokes. A pace away, Dock, his horse and friend, snorted impatiently and shook his mane.

Close to the other wheel up the same side of the wagon, Mary, Charlie, and Roy still slept on an old featherbed, the quilt half covering Charlie whose open mouth reminded Andrew of an upturned catfish's.

As Andrew looked up at Mabel, the mental picture of a green paradise was quite a contrast with the flat, nearly barren land surrounding this family.

He had been wrapped in the coziness of a dream.

Standing up beside the wagon, Andrew began grappling with the practical demands of the day.

"I'm so hungry, and so thirsty," Mabel said.

Giving his daughter a dipperful of water from the small barrel at the back of the wagon, Andrew continued to experience a blur between fantasy and reality. Why had he dreamed about a forest? Had he been there before?

Moving to the campfire, stirring its embers, adding dry brush and sticks to it, the flame grew under the tripod, suspended from which a lidded iron pot contained the remains of last night's meal—cornmeal mush—which would be this morning's breakfast. Pushing the enameled coffee pot into the orange embers at the left of the fire, Andrew waited for it to heat up yesterday's brew.

As he and Mabel sat on the ground huddled close to the fire, the sun's rays came straight at them from the east, with only a few scrubby trees between them and the horizon.

Sipping a very strong tin cup of coffee, Andrew's now fully conscious mind again searched for the source of his dream.

The train ride. That was it. Coming back to Abilene on a train, a stranger had described 120 acres of land in Marion County, Illinois, "so beautiful that it's like the Garden of Eden. Why, you could spend the rest of your days there, living off the fat of the land and timber. And it's for sale."

Andrew had shrugged this offer off, saying, "Well, it sounds mighty tempting for me and my family, but I have no money."

Marquis Burns, now no longer a stranger, leaned interestedly forward in the seat opposite Andrew and said in a new, more serious tone, "What about that invention?"

"What about my invention?" Andrew distractedly responded with a puzzled expression on his face.

"You know, that iron you were telling me about," Marquis deftly answered.

"Oh, *that*. Well, I received the papers on that last month: a steam iron powered by kerosene. I sought the patent to protect my invention, but, confidentially, I think the contraption, which has a little kerosene reservoir in front of the handle, is likely to do more than steam out wrinkles—it may catch the garment on fire. You see, for the fire to burn to heat up the water, it must have air. As a result, I have put scallops around the bottom above the sole plate as vents. However, without great care—or an alteration in my invention—fire inside the iron might shoot out the air vents, burning the clothes or the ironer or both. Therefore, my invention, I'm sorry to say, is really not worth much," Andrew explained apologetically.

"I understand what you're saying," Marquis quickly rejoined, "but I'm something of a gambler, and I'm willing to take risks. Tell you what, I'll just *trade* you."

"The 120 acres for my steam iron?" Andrew asked incredulously.

Unsurely, Andrew shook hands with Marquis, who said, "Done!" And that was the end of it.

Surveying the prairie all around him, and whistling softly to Mabel a few measures of "Blessed Assurance," Andrew pondered that important moment which had brought him where he was today, on the way to 120 acres of land he had never seen before. What if it were a swamp full of snakes and rotting trees? What if it were nothing but rocks and boulders? How could I drag my family across three states, not really knowing what's at the end of the trail? I even owe last year's taxes! What a stupid thing to do. Yet, here we are. There's no turning back now, he thought.

Nevertheless, as the sun was interposed by clouds and a few sprinkles hit his upturned face, Andrew felt that the sale on his iron on the train to a stranger was much more unreal than last night's dream of the timber he was heading toward.

April 16, 1890. Stayed in camp till noon then drove 18 miles and camped on a little creek. It has rained most of the day. Wind in the East.

CHAPTER 3
Discards

Groggy and not just a little nauseated, Mary felt every hole and obstruction in the road. From the top of her shoulder blades to the bottom of her spine, she felt jolt after jolt as the wagon lurched along. Because these roads were poorly maintained—if at all—the Knapps often stopped to remove tree branches, dead animals, and discarded items as they journeyed east. For every wagon headed east as theirs was, a hundred were heading west; a common event was meeting and giving way to a west-bound wagon. The farther these wagons went, the less value was placed on the possessions in the wagon bed so that, to ease the burden on the horses, furniture such as chests of drawers, clawfoot tables, and kitchen tables would be dumped out, their owners not even taking time from their headlong trip west to set them upright along the road in case another traveler saw a treasure. Sadly, these were heirlooms, in many cases, that caused an emotional parting as they were dumped out like so much garbage. As the Knapps came around the bend in the road and started down a steep incline, there on its side in the middle of the road was a pump organ; the sight of this made Mary's heart jump, for it was so similar to the one she had left behind in Nora Springs, Iowa, when she married. Of course, rescuing it from its discarded, sunk-in-the-mud-rut state was completely inconceivable—out of the question. Stopping to move it out of the way, Andrew, Mary, and Charlie heaved it out of the blue muck and in so doing accidentally dropped it, fracturing its beveled mirror; although it was actually not a loss, Mary felt saddened for having reduced its worthless state even more.

Bumping along, at an angle with the horizon more often than level with it, Mary and the kids tired of holding on to the frame of the wagon to avoid being pitched out like the pump organ was. Jarred hour by hour to the point of exhaustion, when the group stopped for the noon meal, then Mary's real work began: gathering dead limbs and sticks, filling the water barrel a bucket at a time from a creek, starting a fire, frying some meat, boiling water for coffee…

Charlie fed the horses oats and hay while Andrew greased the axles, which had been grinding ominously for the last few miles.

Mabel and Roy played with a cast-off coffee grinder they had picked up along the road. As they turned the crank in a slow rhythmic oscillation, they sang phrases of "Oh, Susanah," oblivious to the responsibilities of work and chores. Observing their movements and hearing the happiness of their voices, Mary smiled, dropped the fork she was turning the meat with, and took a turn at the grinder handle, never missing a beat of the cadence the kids had established. The irretrievable innocence of youth, she thought, was more priceless than finely crafted pieces of furniture.

April 17, 1890. Started out this morning about 10 o'clock. Camped on the prairie for dinner. This afternoon came over some teriable roads. Went up a terror of a hill. Camped on a little creek. Has been a nice day. Wind NORTH West. Stoped almost dusk.

CHAPTER 4
The Trunk

The wagon needed some attention the next morning since during last night's last few miles a serenade of squeaks and squawks had punctuated the silence of the sky at twilight as the sun, a warm orange hue, dipped into the west behind them. In fact, every revolution of the wheels brought at predictable intervals the raw sound of metal against metal, calling for grease.

While Andrew and Charlie slathered lard on the axles and the centers of the wheels, a blinding sun again drove straight at them.

Shielding his eyes against the glare as he held the lard bucket for his dad, Charlie felt a paralyzing sting on the side of his left palm. Involuntarily he dropped the bucket, splashing its gooey contents in a grotesque splatter on the powdery dirt.

With his usual steadiness, Andrew grabbed him, asking, "What happened, son?"

"Something stung my hand; it feels like needles," Charlie said through teeth clenched against the pain as he wrung his hand in arcs through the air.

At the moment his dad grabbed his hand for examination, the morning light began fading for Charlie, silver streaks flashed in wavy patterns in front of his eyes, and he fell, like a lifeless fencepost, to the ground, bringing his dad down with him.

Mary, toting a water bucket from the creek, saw father and son hit the ground and began running as fast as her short legs would carry her. A short way off, Roy and Mabel, seeing their mother run, got the signal, silently, that something was very wrong and followed their mother with their hearts beating like hummingbirds.

"Been stung or bitten," Andrew grimaced to Mary. Holding Charlie's arm upright, he said, "Bring me something to tie this off with at the wrist."

In a flash Roy leaped into the wagon before his mother could move; he jumped through the front opening of the canvas and flung open the lid of the trunk stuffed with their breakable valuables.

Roy knew time was important with this emergency for he had once been bitten by a small snake and his mother had made a tourniquet of her apron and tied it at his elbow in case poison was in his forearm. In his case, luckily there was no poison from the snake.

Also, Roy knew that he needed to get a cloth that could be tied easily, not a bulky coat or gunny sack.

So, he tossed out of the trunk a couple of bundles to get down to a pillowcase.

By the time Roy sprang to the ground with the pillow case, Charlie was coming to, asking, "Did I pass out or something?"

"You gave us quite a scare, son." Tying the embroidered pillow case somewhat tightly around Charlie's wrist, Andrew asked, "How is your hand now?"

"It still feels sort of numb, and I have a strange taste in my mouth," Charlie responded, "but I think I'm all right now."

At those welcome words, Andrew broke into a smile, saying, "Well, the lard cures squeaky wheels, so let's see what it can do for what ails a human," and smeared the makeshift salve on the boy's swollen hand.

"What do you think it was? A wasp? Deerfly? Bumble bee?" Andrew questioned.

Charlie came back with, "Don't know, Dad."

With the crisis seemingly over, decamping was now in progress. Mary deposited the cooking pot and the tripod in the back of the wagon, her peripheral vision automatically noting disarray in the wagon bed following Roy's search in the trunk. In such cramped quarters—she judged the whole space to be about four feet wide and 14 feel long—everything had its place, and the trunk's contents must go back inside.

So, in the subdued light of the wagon bed, Mary reached for the first quilt-wrapped article, a large oval, her mother's ironstone platter; as her thumb grasped the edge through the worn quilt, a grating, sandpaper-like sound told her that the platter was broken. However, as she unwound the cushioning, much to her surprise, she found the platter intact, except for a small, floating half moon of detached porcelain that a collision with the vertical wagon side had dislodged.

Wrapping it up again, saving the crescent fragment, she turned to the other parcel on the floor, a baby quilt that protected a recent family photograph glued to a thick cardboard backing for stability. Opening this, she inhaled sharply; this large photograph—about a foot square—had been, by the weight of the ironstone platter above it as well as by the wagon's rocky ride, broken in two, a horizontal fracture cleaving in two Charlie's head, baby Roy's neck, and her right arm at the wrist.

Her attention went, as she held the halves of the picture together, to herself in the upper left of the top half, the half that from her waist and from her severed wrist up featured the rest of her. Distracted, in thought, pensive, troubled, irritated, shocked: what word could have adequately described the expression on her face the day this picture was taken? She certainly had had difficulty paying attention to what the photographer was telling them all to do: "tilt your head to the right"; "look to the left"; "look up—no, not you, Mrs. Knapp, you go back to looking to the right; lift your chin, there, that's it"; "A wisp of hair has just fallen over your ear, madam"; "you must hold very, very still, all of you." Yet all that Mary could really pay close attention to were the troubling thoughts screaming in her mind. In the chaos of taking this family picture of Andrew's, Tillie's, and Burd's families, with the photographer positioning and repositioning, was the sick certainty that she was again in the condition no one talked about; the condition that brought misery, pain, and nausea; the condition that called for constant altering of these close-to-the-hips dresses; the condition that she had endured twice already—yes, she was sure she was going to have another baby. All the signs were there—no doctor needed to confirm what she knew so well.

The split photographic image that Mary Knapp held in her hand out on this lonesome, barren Kansas prairie brought back the stupor of that morning in 1887 when she knew her third child, Mabel, was on the way. She remembered that as she had fastened Charlie's shoes that morning, she used his buttons and the hook as a pro tem abacus: she had calculated that at the current frequency—married in 1882, Charlie born in 1883, Roy in 1885, and Mabel to be in 1888—she would have 13 children by the time she was 50!

Looking down at the likeness of herself three years ago, she wistfully thought how she and Andrew had changed.

This picture, this link to the past and to her husband's family, was special to her, and she was disappointed that it, like the platter, had suffered a symbolic injury.

Mary's mind, returning to the present, was at once saddened and dizzied and sobered by the rapid sequence of events since 1882 when she and Andrew had married and had settled into domestic life in a setting that offered stability, support, and more-than-adequate projected future income from Andrew's patented invention. His family—his parents and his brothers' and sister's families—had graciously embraced her into their close-knit world, and she had seemed to have continued the somewhat genteel lifestyle she had left behind with her parents in Iowa.

Mary's Iowa upbringing had been one of comfort, not exactly one of wealth, but definitely not one of need. Her family was composed of farmers, not sharecroppers, but up-and-coming farmers who owned and loved the land, who improved the land, who grew on the land what the markets called for, and who hired help that was content with a small fraction of the crop and a place to call home.

It wasn't that Mary thought herself *better* than those around her; nevertheless, she knew that the lifestyle she lived—including the clothes, the jewelry, the books, and music, the carriages, the slippers for dancing—were *not* part and parcel of the lives of most members of her community.

At church, for example, she had often felt like she was separate from others and that she was an object of curious scrutiny because of her array of hats, scarves, ruffled dresses, and purses. Even her hair—often elaborately curled with help from the curling iron suspended in the kerosene lamp's chimney—was a source of comment and subsequent discussion at Sunday dinner tables. Clipped phrases such as "coiled like a spring" and "real? I don't think ..." made their way to her hearing as she shyly and demurely took her place in the Stevens family pew.

Well, no one could hint at privilege or vanity now, she thought, not if anyone could see her in the back of this covered wagon, wearing her soiled calico dress and serviceable muddied brogans, her black hair disheveled and floating about her ears, her hands and fingernails blackened by the fire's soot, all her possessions, few and forlorn, contained in this narrow space.

The wagon rocked. Roy and Mabel clambered in from the front drawstring opening in the canvas.

"Charlie says he's better, and Dad says we've got to get going lickety split," Roy announced with a big grin. "That home in Illinois is awaitin'."

Mabel, with those deeply expressive eyes that brimmed both with humor and mischief, sidled over to her mother still crouched down by the trunk and rested her chin on Mary's shoulder and collar bone.

"Ma, are we about there?" she asked with that naiveté of a two-year-old that is unconscious of time and distance and how long they sometimes are.

"No, Mabel, not yet, but we'll be in Illinois before you know it," Mary answered, thinking to herself that at least three weeks remained in this journey of 500 or so miles. Hugging Mabel to her warmly, inwardly she condemned herself for every having been anxious and concerned about the addition of this child to her family.

Mary took in a long breath for strength and thought to herself: like the home in Illinois, her husband and her children were the foundation for her future, uncertain though it was.

April 18, 1890. Camped in a beautiful place on a creek. Directed there by a Dutchman. The day has been a lovely one. Better roads than yesterday. Came through Burlingame about 4 o'clock. Have traveled about 30 miles today. Most dark when we stopped.

CHAPTER 5
Expenses

On this fifth day of their journey, at midmorning Andrew gave the reins to Charlie, who at seven was already a skilled driver and handler of horses. Meanwhile Andrew looked over the family's expenses so far: "Tobacco 10 cents. Hay 10 cents, 5 cents, and 5 cents. Bread 25 c. Oil 10 c. Tobacco 10 c. Hay 10 and 10 c. Sugar 25 c. Butter 10 c. Crackers 25 c. Corn 25 c. Prunes 25 c. Tobacco 20 c. Corn and Oats 75 c. Hay 60 and 10 c."

Only five days on the road, and they had already run through $3.70. And at this pace, they might spend more than $25 if the trip took a month or so.

No need to worry about money right now, Andrew told himself. After all, it was nearly impossible to know how many days this trip might actually take.

Andrew had studied a map and had calculated the distance would exceed 500 miles. He hoped to travel at least 25 miles per day, reaching their Illinois home in perhaps 20 days. Yet, he hadn't factored in the weather, road conditions, illness, accidents, or depletion of money.

All he knew for sure was that he had $26.30 left in his coat pocket—period. Expenses above that figure would necessitate selling possessions or working for pay. Both these options being distasteful, Andrew closed his eyes for a second, thinking, "I'll just think on the bright side. Our money will last. It *has* to."

Looking back over the list, he saw tobacco purchases three times for a total of 40 cents, which was less than a tenth of what had been spent. Hmm, a tenth—that smacked of the biblical directions on tithing. And here he had spend nearly a tenth of their budget on dried leaf fragments that saliva softened until they formed a delicious, slick ball that nested in the pocket of his left cheek, the intoxicating flavor absorbed by the taste buds, and the amber spit-juice combination expelled from the filled reservoir of the left side of his mouth toward the roadside. It was a luxurious ritual. However, the prairie winds being unpredictable, sometimes surprise gusts of wind would catch this projectile spittle and toss it back at Andrew's face or splay it on the side of the wagon's canvas top in a less than artistic arrangement as the goo slid obscenely downward tear-like.

I must do my best, Andrew thought, to shield my sons from this habit.

At the same moment, Charlie's mind, too, was pondering an important matter; he was working a small tobacco leaf with his tongue against his cheek, savoring its texture and flavor. Over the past two months, after initial nausea, he had grown to look forward to a small chaw now and then when he felt it safe to sneak a fragment or two from his dad's tobacco pouch. The only problem he had was choosing judiciously just the right moment to spit, for he couldn't risk anyone, especially Roy and Mabel, finding him out and exposing him to retribution. Twice this morning he had been forced to swallow in the absence of a discretionary opportunity to rid himself of the juice. Now, somewhat green at the corners of his mouth, he waited for just the right moment to be undetected to spit. And once this morning his dad had intently stared sidewise at him, seeming to watch his tongue working in his right cheek. Did he suspect him?

Sitting next to Charlie in the wagon seat, Andrew continued studying expenses Mary had meticulously recorded in her little 4 by 6 bank deposit book. He noted that the horses and wagon upkeep were costing the most: over $2 already for feed and oil. He couldn't begrudge that expense, though, for the two horses were the means of conveyance to their new home. Even at that moment, the horses were straining through a boggy stretch of road, the wheels sunk in a foot of mud.

To Andrew, "Our new home in Illinois" seemed today only abstract words. His old world behind him, his new world yet unseen, Andrew looked at the horses, their muscles severely stressed in the mud that sucked at their hooves, and thought that just five days ago he and his family knew all the comforts of a nice home, yet today they were heading east—against the westward flow of wagons and perhaps east against good judgment. He wondered, did Moses go east—or west—to the promised land, or did he wander aimlessly 40 years in the middle of nowhere? Andrew certainly understood the wandering in the middle of nowhere idea.

Spitting speculatively over the right wagon wheel, Andrew wondered if, his Canaan would be full of giants or milk and honey? Time and miles would tell.

Meanwhile, Charlie, green at the gills, his stomach queasy and churning, snapped the reins and urged the team up a substantial hill, dying to spit.

April 19, 1890. Camped tonight about 1 mile West of Baldwin in the timber. Has been a nice day.

CHAPTER 6
Roy

Sitting in the shadows the pulled-tight canvas at the front of the wagon made, Roy listened to his brother and dad inches from him. They talked about bends and mud holes in the road, they pointed to vultures circling a horse carcass off to the left, they discussed cumulous clouds hovering overhead, and—after reviling the evils of chewing tobacco—speculated on what their home in Illinois would be like.

While Charlie was tall for a seven-year-old and was entrusted with adult jobs, Roy, two years younger, was short and often overlooked when it came time to unhitch the horses, rub them down, grease the axels, and carry the feed. Likewise, it seemed to Roy, his mother tended to go about her cooking duties alone, not considering him as a helper.

In fact, Roy was actually eager to help, eager to be asked to help, and yet seen, he thought, as too young by both his parents.

Reaching up to his neck, Roy tried without success to get the scratchy wool fabric of his coat collar away from his neck. In a quick shift of the wagon, a chorus of suspended clanging iron skillets and kettles sang out in the semi-darkness of the wagon's interior. At the same shift in weight, Roy felt the wool clamp back down on his bare neck like barbed wire. Reaching to disengage it again, Roy noticed a quick turn of Charlie's head and a volley of projectile spit fly to the wagon's left.

It appeared to Roy that Charlie spat while his dad's head was down examining the expense tablet in his lap.

Personally, Roy could not understand the lure of tobacco. He had such a chaw himself yesterday and had spat it out within 15 seconds.

But, if tobacco was what it took to be more grown up, noticed, and respected, then tobacco it would be; he would make himself learn to like it.

It was Charlie and Andrew who led the makeshift church services that morning, passing out the bread and water as communion, offering the prayers of thanks for the health and safety thus far on the trip.

It was Mary, holding little Mabel, who stirred all five to sing "Abide with me, fast falls the eventide" and "Amazing grace, how sweet the sound."

It was Dad who stood and gave a testimony to God's love and protection for this little family wandering in the wilderness, as it were, trying to find their new, promised home.

It was everybody but Roy doing everything noticed and important every day.

Perceptive, intuitive, instinctive, precocious: all could describe Roy. As such, he realized that his mother and dad daily planted false optimism on their faces, when, in their thoughts and in the seats of their hearts, they were as homesick for Abilene and as unsettled about what they would find in Illinois as he was. He would have welcomed a heart-to-heart talk about these feelings that his parents thought he was too young and immature to have.

However, Roy *knew*. He knew that his Grandpa Knapp had tried to bribe Andrew not to leave Abilene both with money and with the promise of a new life buying and selling cattle in Abilene markets. Roy knew that Grandma Charity Knapp had dominated and nearly suffocated his mother, who was herself a strong-willed woman. He remembered one day when his mother, he, and Mabel were walking home after an especially tension-filled afternoon with Grandma Knapp, Mary had said, to the air seemingly, "Oh, that *woman* ... !" with despair in her voice, and Roy *knew* exactly what she meant.

Roy knew that both his mother and dad now wanted to prove themselves to be a strong couple that could independently face and conquer the unknown, free of the constraints of established parents and in-laws. And Roy knew that his time of contribution to the family would come. He knew.

Sunday, April 20, 1890. This is Sunday eve. We started out this afternoon. Come 20 miles. We are camped on a creek. Not a very good place. Has been a nice day.

CHAPTER 7
A Surprise

Walking in the mud and mire, Mary tried to ease the load on the horses as they heaved against the mud, pulling the wagon eastward.

For about an hour, Mabel had skipped along by her side, but as the mud collected layer by layer on her shoes which got heavier and heavier, she began to whine, begging to be carried.

Mary answered her by yelling to Andrew up ahead, "Yooohooo! Stop the wagon so we can rest and scrape."

"Scrape" meant sitting down on last fall's leaves and twigs along the road, dislodging the clay deposits on their shoes with a tree branch.

First, the bottom of the shoes, next the sides, then the tops were attached by the stick held on both ends like a coping saw.

The trouble was, a new shell of mud would, within a half mile, replace the mud just scraped away. However, without periodic stops, the shoes, laden with mud, could exhaust the walker and cause leg cramps. Another possibility was walking out of the shoes and plunging into the mud barefoot.

Cleaning her brogans, Mary noted that the mud had different colorings in it, mostly brown and rust-colored, but now and then gray like a dove's feather or black like a lump of coal. The consistency varied, too, by the mud's content: some mud as sloppy as oats and water, some nearly as thick and as sticky as beef tallow.

Mary picked up Mabel to carry her for a little while at least. Behind her she heard the plopping noise of a horse, just one, which was a rarity on this road.

"It won't be easy for that horse and rider to pass us on this vine-choked road where we've barely room for the team and wagon," she thought to herself.

The closer the rider got, the more she could tell he was singing. Was it "won't you come out tonight"? Why, yes, it seemed to be that refrain, "Buffalo gal won't you come out tonight and dance by the light of the moon."

That was a tune her dad had taught her and her brother when they were just kids in Nora Springs, Iowa. He would sit on the back porch on the cistern, sing that song, and keep time with his palm on the guttering that came down from the eaves into the cistern.

In her memory, Mary could see that two-story house with three porches, one of them two stories, as she plodded along.

And as she slugged along through yet more mud that began to weigh her down, she shifted Mabel to her left hip, cupped her right hand over her eyes, and peered at the approaching man on horseback.

This man, like her dad, had a powerful tenor voice that carried well through the air. And this rider was keeping time by slapping the side of the saddle with his right hand.

The sound of the voice grew stronger and stronger until the man, removing his broad-brimmed hat, came up beside Mary and Mabel, saying, "Hi, Sis," at which point Mary very nearly fell sideways in the mud with Mabel.

Not believing her eyes or ears, Mary shot back, "Lee?"

Lee Stevens, her only sibling, had lived at home, Mary's childhood home in Nora Springs, Iowa, caring for their mother, Mary Ryckman Stevens, until she died of a stroke in 1886, after which he had moved to Abilene to be near his only relative, his sister Mary.

Lee was a big reason Mary had not wanted to uproot and move to Illinois, for after two years when her brother had found work grading cattle in the auction house in downtown Abilene and had bought a house of his own, prepared to spend the rest of his days near her, she had announced in 1889 that she and her family would be moving away the next spring.

"Lee, what in the world do you think you're doing here?" Mary asked, excited though anxious. Being her only link to her upbringing, Lee had always been good for Mary, brought out her good nature, made her laugh, and gave her a sense of peace, that all was right with the world.

But this appearance was sudden, unplanned, perhaps rash. She was confused at this, too.

"It's like this, Sis. Last week when you all left, I was all steeled up to bear you leaving. I didn't come to see you off because goodbye might have pumped up the tears. Heck, I might have begged you to stay. Well, now, the days have passed, and I've felt as unwanted as a skunk at a wedding. I've thought of you, Andrew, and the kids and nothing else night and day. So the only solution I could see clear was to come and join up with you as you march eastward to this paradise you've bought like a pig in a poke. So here I am, for better or worse, as they say," Lee explained, chuckling.

Plunk, Roy jumped out the back of the wagon's canvas drawstring of an opening, running to Uncle Lee, who grabbed a hand and swooped him up behind him. And that's where Roy stayed the rest of that day, he and his Uncle Lee singing away and swapping jokes.

Mary yelled up to Andrew and Charlie, "We've got another passenger back here," at which Charlie reined in the horses, he and Andrew racing behind the wagon to welcome Lee.

After the commotion, hand shaking, slapping, and joking had died down, Andrew said, "Lee, you've always been good sizing up animals, spotting disease, recognizing stubbornness and independence; estimating market value. Do you think you could apply that judgment of yours to the timber to be harvested and sold in a 120-acre woods in Illinois? Do you?"

"I'll tell you the Lord's truth, Andrew. As long as you folks are nearby, I can tackle anything. Let's head toward the timber," Lee answered, grinning and pointing east.

As the Knapps moved through the mud now, it seemed less a struggle; even the horses seemed to have the energy of oxen as they drew their four-wheeled burden down the road. The difference was that Uncle Lee was now a sharer in their journey and in their new life.

Roy looked up at Uncle Lee as he coaxed his horse past the sign that declared "State of Missouri" and said, "Uncle Lee, were you really sad without us?" to which Lee snorted and answered facetiously, "Shucks, no, I wasn't lonesome. I was just downright fearful that without me you might never find your way to Illinois and just wander all across the earth like gypsies the rest of your lives."

Roy felt good inside, for he knew that, even though Uncle Lee would never seriously say it, he loved his sister and her family more than life itself. He needed them.

In camp that night, not sure whether Andrew would judge Lee's presence as a blessing or a curse, Mary scrubbed the iron cooking pot behind the wagon, using water sparingly since they had not found a water supply that day anywhere.

"Lee has a way of making people feel better, doesn't he, Mary?" he asked.

Mary answered, "He certainly does, although I wish he could choose a less dramatic way of showing up like he did today. It's the same approach he used when he showed up after Mother's death: no warning, no clue, just appeared one day in a different state of the union, with the attitude of 'You were expecting me weren't you?' He can be exasperating."

"I'm glad he's with us, Mary," Andrew said, looking her straight in the eye.

Crawling up into the wagon and hanging the pot on its hook, Mary said back, "So am I."

Monday, April 21, 1890. This has been a nice day. Crossed the line (Kansas-Missouri). A nice country through here. Good roads. Traveled 'till dark trying to get to a creek and failed.

CHAPTER 8
Mabel Lavern

As a butterfly emerges from its cocoon, testing its wings, blinking at the light-filled world it never knew as a worm, so likewise Mabel Lavern Knapp had greeted the universe at birth with her eyes wide open, basking in the sun's glow every day since. Her clear blue eyes surveyed a scene, missing no detail, dazzled by the beauty of life in nature. These same eyes, however, could lock onto a person's eyes and could read the thunderstorms of the brain without effort. Precocious, thoughtful, Mabel, only two, had established her place in the family's heart; they saw her as both knowing and unpredictable, a child that had knowledge yoked with curiosity that could lure her under a fence in pursuit of the purple bloom of a thistle, so pretty yet so menacing. Mabel warranted watching, but her angelic appearance often resulted in her parents excusing rather than chastising her caprices. Who could punish a child with luminescent eyes that stared at your very soul?

On the morning of April 22, 1890, Mabel woke up in the wagon bed, after the wagon's left back wheel dropped into a large hole in the road that Andrew had dodged with the front wheel. The bang of an iron skilled against the hoop frame sounded like a gong to her, and frightened, awake, and disoriented, she began to cry.

Mary, walking alongside her brother's horse, heard her cry and sprang into the wagon from the back.

Just how long Mabel ad understood language was unclear, but she had been speaking since her first birthday, so that when her mother comforted her, reassuring that all was right, Mabel said, through tears, "Scared, scared."

"It's OK," her mother repeated. "I'd been scared, too, if I had woke up to such sound a motion."

The featherbed in her upstairs room back in Falls was all Mabel had ever known to wake up in until this month. Warn, peaceful, predictable, the featherbed was a giant pillow that surrounded her with softness and warmth; this careening wagon bed was certainly no substitute for it in comfort and rest.

Abruptly gusts of wind pounded at the wagon's canvas, distorting its barrel-like shape. Mary and Mabel looked up at the cover that separated them from the elements. From the convoluted shapes the wind made of the canvas, it was as if a huge hand were trying to twist the wagon like a lid being screwed on the threads of a jar.

Suddenly water poured from the sky. Lightning flashed so powerfully that it lit up the daylight.

Andrew and Lee stopped the horses, tying them to a tree, and they, Roy, and Charlie, soaked to the skin, dived for shelter in the wagon.

Being wet and getting wet was a major problem for the travelers that was so different from when they got wet back on the farm, for, on the road, because of space constraints, they didn't have multiple changes of clothing. And once the soaked clothes were removed, they had precious little area to hang them to dry. Because of this, this time the men and boys just huddled in the wagon bed and pulled blankets and pillows around their soaked bodies for warmth. And, riding out this storm could lengthen to several hours—or all day and night.

BAM! The sound of rocks pelting the wagon's cover, like a drumhead, caught them all by surprise. Bushels and bushels of rocks shot out of the sky, sounding like the fire of hundreds of rifles.

After the threatening sounds abated, Andrew, opening the drawstring closure at the back, could see not rocks but hail stones; these lemon-sized balls were riding on a current of floodwater that came close to the wheels' hubs.

An eerie, disquieting stillness came, and all six people looked at the ice lemons floating on the currents of water. What an odd sight to behold. The roadway, totally submerged, ceased to exist. The horses, though tethered, half pranced around, trying to escape the cold and texture of the ice flood.

Standing on the step at the back of the wagon, Andrew scooped up a few hailstones and brought them inside.

"Why, look at that—big as June apples!" May exclaimed. "They sure do make big hail here in Missouri, don't they?"

"Cold," said Mabel, holding a stone; Mary stroked her long auburn hair.

"Me all right," Mabel said, looking into her mother's almost transparent eyes for an assessment of how things were.

Mary pitched Mabel's stone out the back, heaving a crunch-plunk as it landed on a heap and then was sucked under the current.

"Yes, we're all all right, I think, Mabel," Mary answered, thinking that this segment of her life seemed so unreal. Hail storms were something a person should experience in a house or a barn, not out in the open with only cloth between you and the sky.

And what other surreal events lay ahead, she wondered?

At noon, the waters began to recede, dropping the hailstones to the again-visible ground. The horses' hooves and wagon's wheels sounded different all that afternoon as they crunched, crunched, crunched through it all, taking the little band further east toward Holden, Missouri.

Mabel's eyes took it all in; as long as her mom said all was right, then it was.

April 22, 1890. We are camped to night on a creek about 1 mile West of Holden. Has rained all day. Has cleared up to night.

CHAPTER 9
Lee Stevens

Keeping a stiff upper lip, finding humor and hope at every turn of daily living, Lee Stevens had been taught by his dad to never complain. What was the use, he said? Complaining was a waste of time and energy that you could never get back.

Riding through the main street of Holden, with the plop, plopping sound the wagon wheels made of the mud they sucked from the mire of the much-stirred-up street, Lee smiled, enjoying the rhythmic cadence of the wagon, dodging an occasional mud missile hurled at random at him, sometimes a fistful of it flying at an oblique angle higher than his head and then coursing downward to splat in the ankle-deep dirt soup. A near miss to his head caused him to laugh and exclaim, "Whew, that mud cow pie nearly made me a new temporary face!" Slapping his left thigh, he looked up at his sister on the wagon seat and said, "What we need today is some more mud!"

Lee's disposition, so different from his sister's had come directly from his dad. Isaac Stevens' fun-loving ways were a complete mask he cultured in order to escape the relative unhappiness of his existence. And that existence, like it or not, was founded on the complaining ways of his wife, Mary Ann Ryckman.

While Isaac made her life a one of financial comfort—a rarity in Nora Springs, Iowa—she nevertheless was contented with nothing. Her approach to life was "If Only." If Only Isaac would care about her—and he actually did love her although she was unaware of it in her self-absorption—then she could be happy and love him back. If Only the pain in her throbbing temples would cease, then she could more patience and understanding with her children. If Only people at church would speak and be nice to her, then she could speak and be nice to them back. If Only her husband hadn't dragged her from the Boston society scene and forced her to live in Iowa, then she could have appreciated and respected him. In an almost whining and definitely down in the mouth tone, she observed daily that life had not been fair to her and that maybe, in time, her life would take a turn and she could be happy.

In his silent, wise heart, Isaac knew that Mary Ann created her own prison of discontent and that she could not exist outside of it; it was her explanation for all of life's events that she thought were deliberately slung by other people against her happiness.

As father and son, Isaac and Lee, went about their daily chores that consistently yielded an income that kept Mary Ann in style, even though she firmly believed that her lifestyle prevented her from living in style, they communicated with words spoken into the air with heads turned to avoid eye contact that they were fellow sufferers and that they might as well make the best of it all by being optimistic and happy. After all, if you said you were miserable enough, you would be miserable; therefore, if you said you were happy often enough, happiness would come. They operated with this philosophy and it worked for them; meanwhile, Mary Ann moped and moped and yearned for what she didn't have that she rightfully could have If Only. Lee had chosen, along with his dad, to be cheerful by acting cheerful, day by day, and he had literally become what he had at first pretended to be. While he was very aware of his mother's immersion in negativity and despair, he knew that that life was not going to claim him. His mother he paid respect to, but he did not emulate her.

Mary Elizabeth, his sister, was another matter, however. Growing up, she wanted to do the impossible: to please her mother and lift the heavy curtain of depression that her mother swathed herself in. Yet, try as she might, Mary Elizabeth could never quite "get there" in her quest to bring sunbeams into her mother's dark existence. And Mary Elizabeth was enormously entertained by her father and brother, who, with their dancing eyes and eager, euphoric vocal inflections were a constant delight to her. She knew of their conspiracy to be happy, and she partially shared in it, from a distance. Personality-wise, Mary was a blend of her mother and her father, with her father predominating.

Yet her mother's genetic gift of absorbed thought about things that her brother and dad could let bounce off them like hail stones on a tin roof kept reining her in, keeping her from being as well-adjusted as she wished she could be. She would consider small remarks, single words uttered in a peculiar tone, and even unusual facial expressions, mulling them over, sometimes for days: what did Andrew mean by that remark about her supper being memorable? She felt, defensively, that she was doing the best she could do—anyone could do—in the primitive conditions of travel. Not outwardly, but very often inwardly, Mary Elizabeth would brood over words and actions and looks she took to be insulting that had no basis in reality.

But, unlike her mother, Mary Elizabeth did not openly complain but bore things stoically. Her own judge and jury action went on in the silent courtroom of her own mind. When questioned about that "look" she had when she was visiting and re-visiting the private theatre of her consciousness, she would say, "Just thinking, that's all," and let it go at that.

Now there was the matter of Charlie's shoes, his ONLY shoes, the shoes he put up on tree limbs to dry overnight. When the family band had reached Williamsburg and the road conditions were greatly improved, Charlie handed over the reins to his dad and jumped out of the wagon. Being barefooted, his left foot bore down on a small tree limb that caused a howl to come from him, to which Andrew asked, "Charlie, where are your shoes?" and the upshot was that—because doubling back 22 miles to fetch the shoes was not an option—a shoe cobbler in Williamsburg outfitted Charlie with new shoes to the tune of $1.25. This expense, although reasonable, was unexpected and unwelcome to this family on a budget as they traveled over 500 miles to a new home. As a result of this expenditure, and the delay with the cobbler, the last hours of the day were ones of silence. Even Uncle Lee wasn't doing the usual joking and teasing and kidding about it. A tense cloud hung over the weary travelers that evening.

Andrew, Mary, Lee, Charlie—especially Charlie—and Roy kept mute even as they began to set up came and gather firewood.

Even Mable was somewhat subdued as she sensed something wasn't right in the air. Her puzzled blue eyes swept the faces of the others, looking for clues.

Wednesday, April 23, 1890. Has been a nice day. Road good. Are camped about 20 miles West of Sedalie. Came through Williams Burge to day since dinner.

CHAPTER 10
Camped

The tenth day of their journey, Thursday, April 24, 1890, gave them all a new definition of "tired." Because there was no rain, the little group pushed forward with an extra effort to make hay while the sun shone, so to speak.

In Sedalia, Mary found in a general store a small crate of lemons. Dr. Jimmy Harrell, a family friend back in Falls, had told her, "Now, Mary, as you make your trip to Illinois—and even after you get there—you'll being eating what's cheap and easiest to fix: cornbread, biscuits, meat, and water gravy. But we now know that without variety, and especially without fruit, your bodies won't be getting what they need. You might even get sick with scurvy, like those sailors on ships get. So, included things like apples, pears, and blackberries to be safe and well."

Well, that was good advice, but in Missouri April didn't mean apples, pears, and blackberries, except for blossoms.

Seeing the lemons, Mary remembered Dr. Harrell's advice. She scooped up four of them @ four for 10 cents.

Putting her lemons on the counter, the proprietor said, "Ma'm, these came all the way up here on the train from Florida." Handing him two nickels, Mary dropped the lemons in the right pocket of her dress that brushed the ground.

"Oh, and I want a very sharp knife to slice these up and make them go as far as possible with my family," she observed.

"Fifty cents, Ma'm," the grocer said, handing her a brand new paring knife wrapped in newspaper.

"Highway robbery," Mary said, handing over two quarters. She turned, walked through the double doors of the store, and was joined by the three children, all of whom climbed into the back of the wagon.

Andrew switched the horses, and they were off.

The remainder of this day was very much like the previous day, except the roads were drier and easier to navigate. Nevertheless, even the best to travel in this covered wagon on these primitive roads was enough to shake your insides to pieces and jar your spine senseless.

As the day and evening wore on, the usual conversations about where to camp for the night went on, but one that had the required level ground, brush for a fire, and water to drink couldn't readily be found.

After looking for a camp spot until 10:00 p.m., all six travelers were weary and frustrated—not to mention famished—for they had gone two hours beyond the usual shut-down time in the dark. This required two kerosene lanterns to be lit and held by their bails by Andrew and Lee on the seat. Still it was a risky business because it was impossible to see beyond the noses of the horses.

This uncertainty that surrounded night travel made most travelers, except those on the railroad, call it a day at dark. Andrew had chosen to begin this move on April 20 because of the longer days and milder temperatures.

Not only was night travel difficult, the kerosene for the lanterns was expensive and space consuming.

Night in 1890 was—except for a campfire or fireplaces and kerosene lamps in homes—a complete, velvety darkness.

Trying, in the dark and in unfamiliar territory—to find a place to stop for the night made Andrew extremely nervous; like his wife and her brother, he had grown up in a house with comforts; this nomadic life, though temporary, had no charms for him. He and Lee finally agreed on a spot, only to find they had nearly gone headlong into Please Creek, which they couldn't see. In addition, they were so near the railroad tracks that when the trains raced east and west, everyone work up or stirred fitfully.

At about daybreak, around 5:15 a. m., Mary and Roy were wide awake after the fourth train headed west, shaking the ground beneath them. In hushed tones, they spoke of the dream that continued to draw them east every day.

"Mother," Roy said, "will be have feather or straw beds in Illinois? I never want to feel the ground under me at night as long as I live."

Mary answered, "Roy, I hope, in time, that you have a warm, dry bed and a full stomach, both of which are lacking here. In Illinois, I think our new life will be better than our old one."

The two lay on the uneven earth of Missouri: no mattress, no fireplace for warmth and cooking, no table and chairs for eating, no roof to ward off rain and sun, no place to call home except that home that they would have to create, by hand and grit, when they reached their destination, which seemed a continent away at the moment.

For a time, between trains, both mother and son stared up at the barely lightening sky and tried to envision that home that would be.

In this tranquil setting, when all the world seemed asleep, the thickets, trees, roadway, and even the creek were all alive with animal sounds, each distinguishable by its characteristic movement and body mass: swish, duh dot, duh dot, went a trio of deer, beating a retreat from foraging to get to their homes for day rest; a stick broke and leaves scattered underneath a possum as it bared its teeth under its cone-like nose and lumbered and plodded back to its young, kuh thump, kuh thunk; "Whooo, whooo, whooo are you," asked an owl perched high in its watch in a cherry bark oak; smaller birds' wings thrashed, barely audible, as cardinals, sparrows, blue jays, and whippoorwills moved from limb to limb in an old pin oak that had presided at the edge of this creek decades before Mary and Andrew were born. The two Knapp horses joined in the symphony, moving their heads left to right. Snorting, and taking prancing, mincing side steps to the melody the birds' shrill voices seemed to send up to God as their morning offering.

The world was coming alive. And the sextet would soon be on its way, shielding their eyes as they headed directly east into the morning sun.

April 24, 1890. Have come about 40 miles today. Came through Sedalia. Drove 'till almost 10 o'clock before we could find a place to camp. Then drove into a place where we had to stop almost in a creek and a very poor place near the R. R. in Pleas Creek.

CHAPTER 11
The Jewelry Box

Rain, rain, and more rain. Tired to the bone from Thursday's long day of travel, everyone was awakened by a strong rain that immediately drove them into the wagon clutching about them their blankets and rolled-up clothing as makeshift pillows.

In that six by fourteen by six confined space, six people stood, half wound up in their wet bedding. Raindrops ran off their faces and drops, tear-like, hung to their noses, earlobes, and shanks of hair.

The practical problem of drying the wet items presented itself next. Obviously stretching blankets and clothing from tree limbs was not feasible. For now, Mary told them all to fold their things and put them in the back left corner of the wagon bed and wait for a break in the rain.

That break never came as it steadily rained all day and evening, a cold rain that you could see your breath in.

What to do, what to do. Roy and Charlie darted out into the rain, soon returning with two sticks as big around as shovel handles, and began to whittle. Charlie was intent on fashioning a walking stick like Grandpa Knapp had back in Falls. Roy, shaving away at the wood beginning on the largest end, announced that he was making a likeness of Uncle Lee's rifle but that he wasn't sure about how to turn our the trigger. Wood shavings shot out of the back of the wagon intermittently.

Sitting up front, Andrew and Lee decided to wile away the time with the highly profitable and respectable activity of chewing tobacco and spitting out the canvas drawstring opening. This worked out well for a time until Andrew heard his projectile of spit make a ping sound on iron. He had missed the wagon seat but had hit the inside or outside of the cooking pot. Mary heard it, too, saying, "And now, Andrew, we're to season our next meal with tobacco spittle?"

"Sorry, Mary. I'll get rid of it," Andrew replied and jumped out in the rain with a rag to smear up the spit.

From then on, a competition arose between Andrew and Lee: who could spit the farthest and not hit the wagon or the iron kettle.

For a long time, Mabel had been entertaining herself with her Mother's sewing basket, humming while she examined the threads, needles, scissors, buttons, pins, buckles, and thimbles. One article at a time she took from the basket and placed in orderly rows on the wagon floor. Soon a full battalion of thimbles, belt buckles, and spools were at attention as if prepared for a parade march.

These entertainments were a gift of the cold rain, for the wagon was still, incapable of moving, and no one need anticipate a big swaying jerk that would displace them and their objects of play.

Nothing moved.

Mary, dropping to her knees, opened her trunk, the one containing the chipped platter, the broken-in-half Knapp family picture, and the extra blankets and quilts.

She and her mother had pieced and finished a quilt that had taken a full year to do; this quilt was the item neatly folded on top, so Mary gave a tug at the first layer of folds then grabbed the back to keep it from coming unfolded. She had forgotten that, as a precaution, she had wrapped this quilt around her jewelry box. Unwinding the quilt, admiring its green, yellow, and white Drunkard's Walk pattern, the jewelry box fell out, its bottom and hinged top jackknifing and spilling out all the contents on the rough wagon floor. At this action, Mary took in a quick, surprised breath, for it seemed that her whole life came symbolically spilling out of that box.

That wooden, enameled black box her parents gave her on her 15th birthday was not worth much in money, but in sentiment it was a treasure to her now 17 years later.

In dimension, the box was maybe 6 by 5 by 1½ inches. The top had painted on it in goldish brown some branches and leaves of an oriental-looking tree coming up out of the right bottom corner and growing to the left, dotted whimsically in four areas with blossoms fashioned of Mother of Pearl.

Mary loved to hold the box to the light and rotate it at different angles to get the iridescent effect of the Mother of Pearl, derived from the shell of the mussel. It seemed these blooms took on life with the pink, lavender, silver, and yellow color patterns that shimmered as the light reflected on them.

Picking up the box, she ran her forefinger along its top edges, noting how time and use had worn off the paint, revealing the butterscotch wood beneath. On the top were also five small teardrop spatters that were reminders of painting the bedroom ceiling of their home in Falls as newlyweds.

Tracing down the front with her ring finger, Mary came to the diamond-shaped lock mechanism with a keyhole resembling the silhouette of a lady. Funny, she thought, that I never used the key since I was afraid I'd either lose it or it wouldn't budge the lock, necessitating smashing the box. With this uneasiness, I eventually lost the key, but that was just as well.

Except for now—the unlocked jewelry box had been upset, and pieces of her past lay in a confused heap on the floor.

One by one, Mary began to pick up her treasures and restore them in an orderly was to the box, similar to the orderly rows Mabel was creating from the sewing basket. Mary decided to go from large to small so as to organize the things rather than to just dump them in one motion back into the box. Never mind that in a few minutes of rocky travel the effect would be all lost.

First, then, was the tintype, a picture of Mary and her mother taken when she was 19. There she was, standing on the left. Her mother, 5' 9" to Mary's 4' 11", had decided to sit on the right so Mary would the focal point of the photograph and so she wouldn't look so short in contrast.

"Stand straight and tall, Mary Elizabeth Stevens," her mother had said, "and turn your head slightly to the left so that your face won't look so pinched and narrow. We want this picture to look good to that Mr. Knapp of yours."

Mary was actually a very comely young woman, a pretty girl in her own right, who didn't need any special angles or drapery to hide defects. Her mother didn't realize that, never would, but it was true nevertheless. Yet, her mother's constant and indirect picking at her appearance, word choice, attitude, behavior, and choice of young men took a toll on Mary, who, because she could never measure up to her mother's expectations—it was impossible, though she didn't realize it—her self-concept seemed as fragile as an egg shell to her sometimes.

For this picture, Mary Elizabeth Stevens had had a completely new ensemble made by Mrs. McWhimsel who had the dress shop next to the bank in Nora Springs. The dress was closely fitted at the waist, as was the fashion at that time, and then it hung in curvy, crescent folds from there to the ground, accomplished by seams straight down the outer legs. The sleeves were finished off with white lace that hid her wrists.

Lace also encircled her neck and flowed like a waterfall festooning down to her waist. Nora Springs' milliner had created for her a hat: a white derby, trimmed with black, with a fluffy black netting attached to the top and nonchalantly hanging off the back brim. Mary's beautiful black hair was drawn back over her ears, and a curling iron had produced several ringlets that went over her right shoulder, hanging down in front. If—in that frozen, photographic state—Mary had shaken her head over so slightly, her ringlets would have bounced and rearranged themselves, and her dangling earrings would have surely jingled. It was 1877, and her ears were pierced, the tiniest wire going through her ear lobe supporting a bell-like droplet.

As usually, her mother whose apparel had also been handled with like minute attention and expense, looked glum and unremarkable. No hat graced her head—she had a headache—no earbobs swung from her lobes, but her hair, parted in the middle, was a cascade of beautiful ringlets as big around as a cigar. Her flat lips emitted not even the suggestion of a smile on her stony, martyred face. She crushed a handkerchief between her hands in her lap.

Mary snapped back to the present and placed this picture in the upper right corner of the jewelry box. So many years, so much had happened. Her youth was gone; her mother was dead.

Next in the box, Mary put mementos that were part of the photograph: her pierced, bell earrings, the pin that held her lace at her neck and bodice, two Mother of Pearl buttons from the front of her dress, a fold of back ribbon from her hat, her hat pin that had kept her hat at just the desired angle, the brooch that held the layers of her mother's lace in place, and her mother's wedding ring, barely visible in the picture.

It was a rare thing to sit and meditate on the past, what with the demands of daily living omnipresent, but on this one day, prevented by rain from proceeding east, Mary had, through her jewelry box, taken a trip, not forward but backward, in time to her upbringing. She looked at her dress, her hands, and her wet, matted hair and thought to herself—as always, just to herself— how she had left her almost fairytale life—in which she took privilege and advantage as the normal course of things—and had established another comfortable existence in Kansas with her husband, his family, and their children.

What, in Heaven's name, then, were they doing by heading, in a most primitive way, to a place they'd never seen to start over?

Friday, April 25, 1890. We are camped tonight in the timber about 1½ miles from clear Creek East. It commenced raining before we got up and has rained all day. It is a cold rain. We have a big fire by the side of the wagon and are comfortable.

CHAPTER 12
Water, Water

Rain peppered the covered covered wagon on the morning of the twelfth day of their migration.

The family had gone to bed early the night before and had listened to the peck, peck, peck of the rain on the canvas. They had decided that sleeping on the ground, as they usually did, was out of the question.

Pairing up, Mary slept with Mabel snuggled up to her, Andrew slept on his side with Roy close to his back, and Lee and Charlie slept on their backs, stretching their long legs at a diagonal to make room for them.

As was the custom, Andrew told, when everyone was under the blankets, a bed tale, as he called it, this one about their Grandpa Knapp—Alexander Van Peter Knapp—whom they had left behind in Kansas.

As rain pelted the canvas, Andrew's low, mellow voice sounded in the darkness. "Grandpa Knapp was born in McKean County, Pennsylvania, far, far away from here.

"When he was nine years old, his parents loaded up all their belongings and all 12 of their children in a boat and floated down the Ohio River and up the Mississippi River to Belleville, Illinois, in St. Clair County, near St. Louis where we're going to be in a few more days.

"The mosquitoes in Belleville were so huge that a flyswatter wouldn't kill them; you needed a scoop shovel or a two-by-four. And, to add to that, malaria, a disease carried by mosquitoes, got so bad and so many people all around them were dying of it, that Grandpa's mom and dad and all 12 children jumped on another big old boat and sailed up the Mississippi to Rockford, Illinois, but his mom and dad weren't satisfied there either, so they uprooted again in a year and went to Rock River, Illinois, where they stayed during your grandpa's teenage years. Eventually, Grandpa got sweet on your grandma, Charity Hooker, they got married and had three sons—one of them me—and a daughter, your Aunt Till.

"Then, just like us, your Grandpa and Grandma Knapp pulled up stakes again and moved to Nora Springs, Iowa, about 20 years ago, and then moved again to Falls, Kansas, in 1877. I'm telling you all this so you can understand that you have come from wandering people. And when we get to Belleville, the Knapp family will have come full circle—counterclockwise—in 1890 back to where they started out in 1838. Now isn't that an interesting story, kids?"

"Dad," Charlie said, shifting onto his side, "could we go to sleep now?"

Crestfallen, Andrew said, "You mean, you're not interested in hearing your family history and where you came from, even when you are a part of the continuing story?"

Charlie answered, "Goodnight, Dad."

In the silent dark, Mary had smiled to herself, thinking she had had much the same attitude when her dad and grandma had told stories of her grandfather, William Stevens, who had a colorful past and had died in 1871. The picture of this William that Grandma had repeatedly thrust in her face repelled her; he looked just like a dead man propped up in a chair for the photographer to shoot at his own funeral. His eyes might as well have been glass for all the life in them, and his beard obscured most of his face and made him look scary and weird. The picture was so ancient, in fact, that the cardboard backing smelled of decay; and the writer of William's birth and death dates had used white ink!

Andrew was always crushed when the children were not ignited with the same flame of interest he had in his family stories from long ago. But Mary knew that that interest and appreciation would come later to the children. They just lived for the moment; the past and the future were dim regions not real to them at the present time.

Mary's mind wandered to a more pressing problem: food. The family had existed on bread, butter, crackers, cornbread, and a little meat for the past 11 days, with a few beans and lemons thrown in for variety.

Now that they had basically sat still for two days, the food supply was critically low, with no town close by.

Water had been a different matter, however. They had been fortunate to find wells and creeks, where they drank freely and without fear of contamination. And in these rains, Mary had put two wooden bowls on the wagon seat to collect drinking and cooking water.

So, they might have to go a little hungry, but not a little thirsty.

At daybreak—no one had any idea of what time it actually was, for Andrew's pocket watch had run down the first day of the journey, and he hadn't met anyone with the right time to re-set it—Andrew and Lee yawned, stretched, and looked out the back of the wagon at the ominous, gray approaching clouds in the west.

"Let's get some more wood for the fire before even more rain gets here," Lee suggested.

The two brothers-in-law climbed out and began scavenging for fallen limbs and logs. Since they were camped in timber that looked untamed and uncut, finding fuel was easy: it was on the ground waiting for them, and there was lots of it.

Tossing sticks on top of the embers, Andrew easily got a blaze going. Lee added some bigger pieces later. The fire was close enough to the wagon for warmth but not so close to be a fire danger.

From the first day of all this rain, Mary still had wet bedding and clothes to dry, so she began hanging up what she could from the wagon hoops overhead. To put it out in the open air meant instant soppiness.

As the day warmed up in the afternoon, the men and boys stripped off their clothes and bathed, as best they could, in the creek. Of course, the water was uncomfortably cold, and they didn't tarry long in it.

When they finished, they took a circuitous, half-camouflaged route back to the wagon, where Mary, averting Mabel's eyes, handed them rags to dry on.

This was the best they could do, hygiene-wise.

Mary was much too modest to attempt a creek bath for herself and Mabel. They made do with a spit-bath, that is, washing with a wet rag. Mabel, once, had asked her mother about this practice, "Mom, in a spit-bath, do you wash everything?" to which Mary replied, "I guess you could say that."

Water, water everywhere.

April 26, 1890. Still camped in the Timber. Have had a nice big fire all day by the wagon. Have been drying the bedding. Has rained most all night and day by spells. Have traveled 1 ½ miles since Thursday. Today is Saturday.

CHAPTER 13
Church

A full moon ushered in a gorgeous dawn. It was Sunday morning. Before the sun was visible, a rosy glow preceded it, blending seamlessly with the intense blue of the sky. Rainbow-like colors, they were. If only the beauty of the morning could be matched by the desirability of the road surface, which more closely resembled a hog wallow than a thoroughfare.

On this, their second Sunday as immigrants, Mary looked to the west—a hilly expanse of trees as far as the eye could see; no buildings or other humans were in sight.

Back in Falls, according to her old Sunday morning routine, at about this time of day she would have been finishing the breakfast dishes in the zinc sink. Andrew and the boys would have been, by now, putting on their Sunday clothes: suits constructed by the tailor in Abilene. Each Saturday Mary attacked these suits with a hair brush to dislodge any lint, stray thread, or dirt. The white shirts they put on she had boiled on the stove, rinsed in a tub of cold water, and then dipped in a tub of starch before she pinned them to the line—inside or outside—to dry. Ironing these shirts was a torture for Mary; she had to heat the heavy iron on the cook stove and then work out the creases as long as the heat held out in the iron—that is, until Andrew's invention, which he had created just for her, knowing the difficulty and strain ironing was for her. His patented steam iron, fueled by kerosene, spewed steam in a little cloud from the sides of the iron. This had made ironing actually only slightly more bearable to Mary, whose weak arms and wrists ached after hours of ironing shirts, dresses, trousers, and handkerchiefs, no matter what iron she used. But because Andrew had gone to the extreme of inventing, patenting, and manufacturing the iron, she flattered and humored him, not telling him ironing was, after all was said and done, still, for her, a trial.

As the sun moved about halfway from horizon to straight overhead, Mary thought, "They're sitting in their pews now—Grandpa and Grandma Knapp, Aunt Till, Uncle Burd, all of them waiting for the service to begin. Cousin Clemmie has adjusted her stiff ruffles around the organ stool; she's poised with her buttoned boots on the organ pedals, waiting for Roscoe Sam, the song leader, to begin the worship. Soon Clemmie will begin pedaling, riding that organ just like it were a bicycle, forcing air into the bellows to create the shrill tones of the reeds."

Closing her eyes for a moment, it felt like she was really there in that one-room church. She could smell distinctly the hymnal pages, a close, dank, unaired smell that mixed with the aromatic pine wood of the pews. Roscoe rose, Clemmie began playing the last few bars as an introduction, and all the people joined in singing "When I Can Read My Title Clear." Funny, but at that moment she remembered hearing that that song was President Lincoln's favorite hymn.

She opened her eyes. This Sunday morning, the second Sunday away from home, tore Mary up inside. The family's makeshift service of singing "Amazing Grace" and "Abide With Me," just like last Sunday, was a poor substitute for a real worship service. Here they stood, dirty, disheveled, in the middle of the road, joined hands, and prayed.

And Mary was worried, too, about Andrew. He was not one to advertise personal or physical problems, but for the last few weeks, Mary had begun to notice things about him that, collectively, greatly concerned her. First, he had begun to nod off to sleep at any time of the day, even when he was driving the wagon. Questioned about it, Andrew replied that he wasn't sleeping well at night. Yet, it was Mary who battled sleep, and she had never seen him awake in the night.

Vision also seemed to be a problem for Andrew. Mary had seen him rub his eyes and squint to see beyond the horses. He would sometimes bat his eyes while trying to focus on something in the distance.

Then there was thirst. It seemed Andrew could not get enough to drink. During the last three days, Andrew had drunk, dipperful by dipperful, all the water in the galvanized can.

What could all this mean? Mary didn't know, but she was sure of one thing: sleeping, sight, and thirst were all changes in Andrew that surely meant a change in his body, a change that wasn't for the good.

Andrew's brother, Robert, had had an unquenchable thirst that he had gone to the doctor about. However, even though the doctor said his thirst was abnormal, he gave no cause or treatment for it. Maybe Andrew had what Robert had, an undiagnosed ailment. Maybe when passing through St. Louis she could suggest seeing a doctor to Andrew, that is, if they had enough money left then.

What with the homesickness for their church and the anxiety about Andrew's health, Mary only half paid attention as Andrew led the family in prayer, giving thanks for their well-being and for Jesus Christ's sacrifice for them, and asking God to give them strength to complete this trip and establish a new home.

Mary wondered about churches in Illinois. Would there be a church close to their timber? If so, would it be Methodist? Baptist? Presbyterian? Catholic? Would it ever be possible to feel at home in a church again?

And, first and foremost, she wondered, "What is wrong with Andrew?"

Sunday, April 27, 1890. This has been a beautiful day. The roads are very bad. Have come about 10 miles this afternoon. Have camped in the timber. It is Sunday.

Mary Stevens and her mother, Mary Ann Ryckman Stevens

Matilda Knapp Williams and Andrew Knapp, standing; Mr.
Williams and unknown woman, seated.

Mary Stevens Knapp

Mary and Andrew Knapp

Charlie Knapp

Andrew Knapp, holding Charlie Knapp

Roy Knapp

Charlie Knapp

Knapp family in 1887. Seated adults are, from left, Andrew
Knapp, Matilda Knapp Williams, and Miles Knapp. Standing
adults are, from left, Mary Knapp, Estey Burdette Knapp, Mr.
Williams, and Mrs. Knapp. Andrew Knapp is holding Charlie
Knapp, left, and Roy Knapp. The two boys in the foreground
are unidentified. The three children to the far right are May,
left, Alta, and Lucy Knapp.

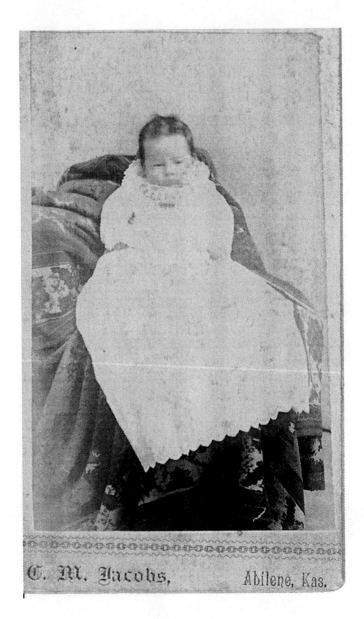

C. M. Jacobs, Abilene, Kas.

Mabel Knapp

Charity Knapp, Andrew's mother

Alexander Van Peter Knapp, Andrew's father

William Stevens, Mary Knapp's grandfather

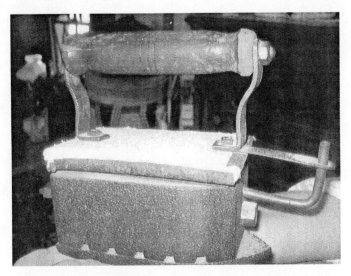

Andrew Knapp's patented steam iron

Destination: the 120 acres of land in Romine Township, Marion, County, Illinois traded for the steam iron patent.

CHAPTER 14
The Train

Andrew, when he was in deep thought, assumed a stance that Mary, Charlie, and Roy knew well: he would stand, fingers just barely touching his trouser waistband, head slightly cocked to the left—with a corresponding slant of his hat—his eyes looking overhead in an almost dreamy state, his stomach slightly pushed forward. When in this posture, he would seem to greeze for many minutes at a time in complete silence. The family had learned to not break this solitude. And it was this silhouette they saw Andrew made as darkness was falling. Andrew stood between them and the railroad tracks, thinking his thoughts, the campfire faintly lighting the backof him with flickering shadows.

"Ma," Charlie whispered, "he's thinking again. Look at him."

Shushing him, Mary said "Now you just leave him be. His head I like a giant clock, ticking away at something eating at him. He'll talk only if he's good and ready."

Charlie and Roy could recognize this posture so well because, seeing their dad do it so often, they had been practicing the same pose when Andrew wasn't looking. As they studied their dad, they inwardly evaluated themselves and concluded that they, too, could stand like that, just so, and think intently.

On this, their 14th day of travel, they were again on a road that bordered the Missouri Pacific Railroad, which was roughly following the path of the Missouri River. Their road had been parallel to the river and to the tracks for the last two days.

Breaking his concentration, Andrew turned around, himself again, and walked back to the campfire, saying, "About 40 years ago, the people of St. Louis started a railroad from their city to the west, hoping to improve trade with distant points. By the end of the Civil War, the tracks had reached Kansas City."

Pausing, Andrew nudged the end of a large tree limb into the fire with his boot. "This was the first railroad west of the Mississippi, and I believe it now goes all the way to California," he said, sweeping his left hand toward the western horizon.

Moving his hands from his waist and linking his arms as if in response to cold, he continued, "I had hoped that we would be making this trip on the Iron Horse. Wouldn't that have been fun? However, train fare for us and all our belongings in the wagon would have far exceeded our $25 budget, which is all the money we have in the world. So," he remarked, turning his head in the direction of Dock and the wagon, "this is the best we can do."

It seemed to Mary he was trying to apologized, that he felt guilty that they were moving by covered wagon, and this actually surprised her, having never considered the railroad. In fact, the railroad rather scared her; it was loud, sooty, and—it seemed to her—so dangerously f st that it couldn't be safe. No, she would much rather entrust her family to a wagon and two horses than to a roaring monster of a train.

Putting her hand in Andrew's, she reassured him, "Andy, I wouldn't get on a train with my family if you paid me!"

Andrew turned and faced her straight, saying, with a tone of ironic humor, "Well, Mary Elizabeth Stevens Knapp, that is a good thing to know, considering our family wealth, which is only dreams."

With his back against the back wagon wheel, Roy contemplated the railroad; it had been on his mind these last two days. When a freighter flew past, shaking the road beneath them, moving with such velocity it seemed it could just leave the tracks, he though the whole thing was fascinating, something powerful and admirable. Oh, if only he could ride one of these trains. He knew his dad had taken brief trips on the train—as a matter of fact, it was on a train that his dad had swapped his patented steam iron for 120 acres of forest in Illinois, which was the reason they were even on this move.

A horse was fine. Roy had learned to ride last year. And the wagon was a nice shelter in a storm. But the TRAIN captured his imagination, thrilled him, made his heart pound and his eyes dance as it raced past.

When he grew up, he knew what he wanted to be: a conductor on a train. However, he kept all this to himself, knowing how his mother felt about trains. If SHE knew about his plans, she would start worrying this very minute. There would be plenty of time for this idea to play out in his life, after they got to Illinois, after they built a housed, after they got rich in the timer, and after he left home for a life on his own.

As the campfire reduced to glowing orange coals and gray ash; as Mary, Andrew, Roy, and Charlie contemplated the railroad; and as Uncle Lee told Mabel bedtime stories about the long ago times of her Great-Grandpa William Stevens during the War of 1812 when the British burned the White House and Great-Grandpa Stevens' unit helped salvage furniture and paintings from the flames in a brigade style of rescue; as all of this happened, the faint vibration of a train rumbled in the distant east, coming closer and getting louder by degrees until when it passed the little family and threw a few chunks of gravel at them from the track bed, they felt small and insignificant in it power and majesty.

April 28, 1890. Camped to night in the edge of the timber close to the R.R. Had bad roads all day but getting better. Come through Tipton and California to day.

CHAPTER 15
Reading

"When I first heard this story, I was a child, and at home I thought of Delilah every time Mother brought out her big sewing scissors. I could just imagine the crisp, metallic sound of the scissors blades as Delilah cut off all of Sampson's hear in his sleep so that he woke up as weak as a cat. Actually, now that I can read it for myself—and for you kids—I know I formed an incorrect picture of this story in my mind, for the Bible actually tells it this way: 'And she made him sleep upon her knees; and she called for a man, and she caused him to shave off the seven locks of his head; and she began to afflict him, and his strength went from him'."

Interrupting, Charlie asked, "What are seven locks about anyway?" to which Mary answered, "He must have divided his long hair into seven big old pony tails so that all the razor man had to do was grab ahold of a lock—or a shock—and shave it off."

"What did hair have to do with how strong he was?" Roy asked, shifting Mabel—who was fidgeting and pulling on her own hair—on his knee.

Mary explained, "This I hard to understand when you're young, but I think this story show us that we shouldn't get the big head ourselves and think that we are strong and all-powerful all by ourselves. Like Sampson—who made things right between himself and God and asked God to give him the strength to push those mighty pillars and bring the big house crashing down on all those Philistines—we should understand that our strength, both in muscle and in mind, comes from the Lord. Sampson prayed, here it says in Judges, "'Lord God remember me, and strengthen me, I pray thee... .' God gave him the strength he needed even though his long hair was completely gone."

Stopping to hoist wandering Mabel up into her lap, Mary continued, "Sometimes people feel they can just do all right alone, that they don't need God, that they can conquer all their problems and can make their lives all better without God. I thought of this last night as the train screamed past our campsite. We are awestruck when we compare that train with all its power to our two comparatively little horses. Today we paid 70 cents to have them shod in Jefferson City. I can't imagine how many thousands, tens of thousands, or hundreds of thousands that train costs to build, fuel, and operate. But, kids, that train is a flyspeck in the universe compared to God's presence and power. Always remember to put your hope and belief in God first. Your true strength for living comes from him. You'll never go wrong doing that."

Mary closed her old Bible, dog-eared, stained with rain, and battered from long use. The kids danced around the campfire and Uncle Lee got in on the chase, causing them to dart left and right to avoid his tag or capture.

How life experiences did alter your depth of understanding of the scriptures, Mary thought. How different and changed the Bible stories seemed after age, difficulty, joy, death, and change of circumstances molded your perspective.

Mary felt lucky that her parents and their parents were Bible-reading church goers who used the scriptures as a guidebook for everyday life. Her mother—in spite of her self-absorption—had always read to her, her sisters, and her brother. And Mary had continued that daily reading—usually at night—with her own children. Oh, sometimes Andrew would read, but it usually fell to her to do it. This inheritance, to her, was a valuable thing to have received from her mother; she vowed that her children would receive it from her. It was her heartfelt wish that her children would pass it on, likewise, to their own children.

In the past few days, since her brother had joined them, Mary noticed that as she read to the children, Lee would stand at the front corner of the wagon and listen. This was special to him, too. He could probably see in Mary's reading, their own mother doing the same decades earlier. Mary thought it would please Lee to take a turn now and then at bible reading. Yes, she would definitely ask him. With his humor and enthusiasm, he could certainly keep the kids' interest.

Mary thought, isn't life a curious journey, with unexpected twists and turns? While today had been perfectly gorgeous weather, she had never seen such uneven, rough country. At times the wagon shook so and lurched so at the unexpected holes, roots, branches, and rocks that she felt sure all of their belongings—and all of THEM—would be catapulted from the wagon in a giant explosion. Days like today, at the end of which Mary felt they had all been shaken loose from their very bones, were a physical and mental challenge. She silently recited, "O Lord God, remember me, I pray thee, and strengthen me."

April 29, 1890. This has been a beautiful day. We have come over the worst country I ever saw. Rough, hilly and woods. Come through Jefferson City this afternoon. Are camped in the timber not far from Osage River.

CHAPTER 16
An Interior View

Another end of another day. Another period of silent contemplation in that familiar stance. Andrew has brushed down the horses tied to a sassafras sapling; his mind is crowded with unwelcome guests as he stands staring at the orange-red sun still half visible on the horizon. All around him is evidence of active life: the horses slightly move, eating the prairie grass; Mary has just added a handful of popcorn to the lidded iron pot suspended by the tripod and chain over the low flames of the fire; Charlie, Roy, and Lee are throwing rocks down the road west, seeing who can throw the farthest in 20 throws; Mabel sits in the dirt and draws a large stick in a semi-circle around her, erases the mark, and repeats the arc over and over.

If it had been possible to enter the consciousness of Andrew's brain with pen and paper in hand to record the events of his life as they really preoccupied his mind and personality— as they took over his concentration—the record of events, topics, and their importances—on paper—it would have revealed a vastly different Andrew than people, including his wife, knew.

All his life, Andrew had kept things to himself. Whether from experiences or teachings or heredity he did this, he didn't know. And why he chose to keep most of the contents of his heart secured in the locked vault of his soul instead of openly sharing them with others was a mystery to him. During his teenage years, he realized that he was different from many people around him, that he kept his private thoughts under lock and key; this practice had developed over 15 years while he was unaware of it; it had solidified before he knew it had; and once he was conscious of its form, his resolve to never reveal his precious inner self was as hard and heavy and unmovable as a granite mountain formed millions of years ago, jutting out of the landscape, the sun's rays glinting off of it. At the Institute of Science at Topeka, he had studied samples of rocks, including granite, and it was then that he made the comparison of his own mind to the hard material rock. While a student in the two-year curriculum at the school, Andrew had excelled, partially because his being to himself availed to him countless, uninterrupted hours of study time, partly because nature fascinated him. Learning classifications of rock and minerals, elements in chemistry, and equations in math—these were private matters that he could prove his knowledge of on paper tests and oral exams. They were safe to him, too, because they were cold, hard facts that didn't require any openness about matters of the heart, no glimpses into interpretation or emotion.

People, though, were different from matter. They could, when you told them things stored up in the deep well of the soul, use the information and give it a new form later. People, he found, could criticize, judge, surmise, and recall words out of context to use against you later. From those released thoughts, people might see you as weak, unintelligent, untrustworthy, unlovable, and unloved, all of which reactions were horrific for Andrew to even fathom. Imagine how weak people would see him if they knew how terrified of water he was: crossing the Osage River on a ferry was so scary to him he was sick to his stomach.

No, it was much safer to keep old and current demons—as he called them—imprisoned, never so much as acknowledging their existence down there.

Yet, sometimes—in spite of his determination and will to prevent them—his thoughts, responses, disappointments, worried, resentments, griefs, expectations, and so on, would clamp down on his mind, controlling it for what seemed like endless time periods. He believed that this was his punishment for concealing the very same things he actually WANTED to talk about—that the fierce chariot races in the arena of his mind actually grew more intense and violent because they had no escape route; they were forced, because of their enclosure in his psyche, to remain there, never to exit the track into the consciousness of real life through their revelation to a human being, always running frantic circles in his head.

Of course, keeping his inner self under wraps exacted a tremendous energy drain on him. It also required solitude, time when his family was justifiably curious about what he was thinking. Yet, to explain to them what he was really thinking about was what he most closely guarded against—even though he conversely wanted to let it go and open the gates—so it was exhausting to him and perplexing to them. If he should open his hear to his family, they would, he thought, see a person they had never seen before: a complete stranger.

Therefore, Andrew contemplated. His thoughts turned to the immediate: how wearing this trip had been. The last 16 days had been pure physical and mental torture. The arduous journey was obvious to all, but Andrew was torn up by both what he had left behind and by what he had yet to see.

All his life, Andrew had had his father to depend on. And in his father, Andrew had a friend, someone whose mind seemed to operate much like his own. Alexander, his dad, had raised him to be independent and had given him a good mind through reading and discussion and through formal education. Until this month, however, Andrew had never been very far from his dad for any length of time. At times, the very idea of selling his steam iron patent for 120 acres and then blindly setting out for it was completely ludicrous; he laughed inwardly and bitterly at his own stupid impetuousness. Another part of him, though, was settled on the idea that at age 34, it was time for him to prove himself, both to himself and to his father, that he could— through smarts, ingenuity, hard work, and faith in himself— make his own life for himself and his family, apart from his dad.

In his intuitive mind, Andrew felt that his dad did not approve of this move of his to Illinois. At their departure, his dad had shaken his hand and said, cryptically, "It is a good thing for people to work, although sometimes they don't want to." Andrew had pondered that sentence long and hard and had never made sense of it. Nevertheless, his father had never said anything directly against his setting out for Illinois; the notion, though, didn't sound to Andrew like one of that dad would ever go for himself.

How could two souls dedicated to keeping emotions absent read each other in emotional times like leaving home for good? How could Andrew be sure of that he wanted and what his dad wanted for him? If was all a mystifying surmise.

Would Andrew even see his parents again? Would his parents ever see him again?

Today had been extremely hard, the terrain being irregular and the roads likewise.

Worse yet was how Andrew was feeling. Unknown to his family—although Mary had been giving him questioning looks lately—he had been having fatigue beyond the ordinary the last month. His vision was somewhat blurred at times. And he was constantly hungry and thirsty. How much of this was due to the strain he was under and how much would have been existing without the pressure and demands of the trip, he had no way of knowing. So, he questioned whether he would even be physically able to clear timber, build a house, dig a well, and make a living for his family in the unknown, unseen place they were heading for. What would happen to his family if he couldn't? Thank goodness for Lee; at least he had him to rely on.

Today, repeatedly Andrew had thought, "Let's turn around and go back." But for now, his resolve had triumphed over his doubt.

On east they would go.

April 30, 1890. Are camped to night about 2 ½ hours drive from Linn. The roads have been worse today than yesterday. Such hills I never saw a team go over before. Crossed the Osage River this forenoon on a ferry. Has been a nice day. Came up a steep hill and camped on top.

CHAPTER 17
Security

Gypsies and the night.

Mary Knapp had always feared them both.

Mary's mother had instilled these two fears in her in two completely different processes.

Gypsies—with their dark skin and eyes, orange and purple scarves, and big hoop golden earrings on both women and men—often camped at the edge of Nora Springs, Iowa, where Mary grew up. Up to six wagons of them at a time would rumble through town, scattering—at the sight of them and at the sound of their cantinas—the decent people who had heard stories of their stealing anything and everything that wasn't nailed down—including children.

Local people, especially grandmas and grandpas, told young children that if they weren't good and well-behaved, the Gypsies would kidnap them and make them eat dog soup. Parents would often—driven to extremes of patience—tell their kids that if they didn't "straighten up," they would sell them to the Gypsies. Admittedly, the two attempts at discipline actually rarely reaped a good harvest of conduct and attitude.

In some adults and children, the Gypsy stories were not much more than entertainment and propaganda, yet others took them quite seriously and reacted to their presence by grabbing their children and their valuables and staying out of sight until the Gypsies moved on. By nature they were nomadic, and, in truth, they did sometimes eat dogs and render their lard for trying; in fact, they would out of necessity eat whatever was at hand, such as a nice fat hen, transformed into chicken and dumplings. In general, Gypsies actually had their hands full with their own numerous children and did not seek to increase their anxieties or indigestion with stolen ones. But, because they were here again and gone, because they looked so colorful and strange, and because a hog or chicken sometimes came up missing from a nearby pen, residents of Nora Springs looked at them with great suspicion and uneasiness.

For Mary Ann Stevens, Mary Knapp's mother, however, just the sight of a Gypsy caused immediate terror in her heart and mind, this reaction forming when she was a youngster. You see, her father, Reynolds Ryckman, who fought alongside her future father-in-law, William Stevens, in the War of 1812, had told her his eyewitness account of the Gypsies, along with the British, looting Washington, D. C. and the White House while both were burning. In great and glowing detail, which naturally grew in emotion and action and heroism over time, her dad described what the Gypsies looked like as the Army, so few in number to guard the capital, watched them clean up like vultures, speaking of their black, malevolent eyes, their pearly white teeth, their bejeweled daggers, their colorful and flamboyant clothing, and their large circular golden earrings that shone as the flames consumed the public buildings. In a word, Gypsies embodied all that was evil and bad.

With her own four children, Mary Ann, when she saw Gypsies in Iowa, felt it was her duty to make them understand the full extent of their jeopardy when Gypsies were around.

After all this indoctrination from her mother, young Mary Stevens became terrified of Gypsies, even though not one incident in her life had in any way confirmed what she erroneously believed to be true about them.

Unlike the fear of Gypsies, which Mary Ann had purposely and directly passed on to her children, the fear of the dark was something Mary Ann had created in her daughter indirectly and unknowingly. To free herself from her four children in the evenings, Mary Ann had ordained—forcefully upholding it as a law—that bedtime for them was 7:00 p.m.

How young Mary dreaded and hated this, especially in the months of shorter days, for she would like alone in the darkness, hearing the slightest rustling, murmur, creaking, or animal noise as ominous. "Who or what is that out there?" she would think in a panic. Was it a Gypsy that might climb the gutter, walk on the porch roof, some through the window at the foot of her bed, and carry her off into a life of slavery? It was too unbearable even to think of. She would bury her face in the featherbed and hold a pillow over the back of her head to stifle the sounds. It never occurred to her that she might seek comfort in her mother's arms downstairs; she knew that if she got out of bed and left her room before morning, her mother would berate and punish her, not to mention that she would make fun of her for being afraid of the dark and imagining things. So, night after night, year after year, she was paralyzed with fear of the darkness that surrounded her, the darkness that she had no control over at all.

From these early experiences, Mary equated darkness with being alone and powerless against evil forces that might seize her at any moment.

As a parent herself now, Mark had sworn to herself that she would do everything in her power to enable her children to react to Gypsies and to darkness with complacence and equanimity. She hoped that to them, Gypsies and the night would not inspire fear.

When the family, on this their seventeenth day on their trek to Illinois, was waiting in Drake for Dock to be shod, and while they were all studying the contents in the front window of Turney's General Store, a caravan of Gypsies passed by headed west. For Mary, if was instantly as if a large hand was gripping her throat and squeezing the breath out of her. Instinctively, her pupils widened and her heart pounded so hard she thought she could hear it. To a passerby, though, this scene was just a man, a woman, and their three children window shopping, a serene picture with no hint of unrest or alarm, so well did Mary control her anxiety.

Thankfully, that caravan of Gypsies was going in the opposite direction the Knapps were headed or Mary would have been constantly apprehensive that the band might be lying in wait to attack them with their daggers.

At the General Store, Andrew handed over $2.10 for supplies: corn, 75 cents; bread, 25; oil, 10; tobacco, 10; meat, 20; hay, 35; and butter, 35. Also, the blacksmith charged 60 cents, and the ferry over the Gasconade River cost 75 cents.

After such a morning of mixing with people, it was an afternoon and evening of the usual solitary travel, the wooden wheels on the old wagon going round and round, up and down over hills and dales.

"I've never in my life seen such peaks and valleys," Uncle Lee remarked after several hours of jostling and being shaken half to death. For a time, Mary, Uncle Lee, and Charlie walked the dirt road, with Uncle Lee's horse tied to the back of the wagon and trotting alone riderless.

At nightfall, having cooked the usual cornbread—with a little ham as a special treat tonight—having cleaned up supper dishes and the iron pot, and having gotten everyone bedded down on the ground, which at this point was relatively level, Mary's mind cast back to the Gypsies at Drake. They scared her at age 32 just as much as they did at age six. And here she was in the dark, again, with only a sliver of a moon overhead.

Funny, she thought in the blackness, how even at this time when almost everything in her life was drastically changing, some things never changed.

May 1, 1890. Camped by the road in the woods. Had quite a time finding water. Traveled all day up hill and down 'till this evening have come onto some level ground which seems like we was among the living again. Crossed quite a river this forenoon on a small ferry. We are about 4 miles from Drake. Had Dock shod there. Expenses: Ferry 75 cents, corn 40, Dock shod 60, bread 25, oil 10, tobacco 10, meat 20, corn 35, may 35, butter 35.

CHAPTER 18
Hospitality

All the comforts of home. All gone.

In this day when agriculture was the primary occupation of the Mid-West, farm houses, both old and new, were a common sight every few miles from Falls, Kansas, to St. Louis and beyond.

The older houses were constructed of roughly-hewn logs set together in the familiar pattern of the Lincoln log cabin icon. Although Andrew, Mary, and Lee were all three under the age of six when Abraham Lincoln went to the White House, their image of Lincoln as the great Emancipator who had been born in a humble log cabin had been later fixed by their parents, all four of whom had cast their votes for him in 1860.

Besides the small cabin that sometimes had a sleeping loft, the travelers also saw the less common two-story log house, with windows at the peaks of the two end gables.

These log homes were rustic and sentimental, harkening back to the days of yore. As the Knapps passed them, smoke from wood fires came puffing out of stone and mortar chimneys.

But things and styles were changing. New homes tended to be no longer constructed with logs stacked as walls but with 2 by 4's and 2 x 6's making a skeleton that was closed in with overlapping horizontal thin boards nailed in place and with the inner walls finished with small strips of wood to which plaster was applied. Like the log houses, these new frame houses were both one and two stories. And while some were rectangular in shape, others were L- or T-shaped.

These new-fangled homes reminded Andrew and Mary of the ten-year-old two-story frame house they had left behind in Falls. Mary could close her eyes and see the peacock printed wallpaper in her parlor; in her mind she could smell the dank, close cool air of the concreted cellar she had access to from her back porch. In a similar manner, Lee could visualize the home he had left in Nora Springs, Iowa, before heading for Falls. This home was also a two-story frame home, complete with a network of guttering that fed into a cistern.

Today, the eighteenth day of their migration, even the most humble log cabin along the road looked homey and inviting, for it stood for permanence and routine, both of which were sorely lacking in this their third week of the trip. Inside all these homes were beds, the crudest of which outshone the wagon bed and the bare dirt in softness. And each home had a table where food prepared on a fireplace or wood stove was set. When the rains came and the wind blew, these homes meant safety and dry clothes.

Instead, the Knapp family was traveling, Gypsy-like, toward the unknown. At times, just finding water to drink was a serious problem for them; the water from a creek was often preferable to the abandoned wells they found, with scum, algae, tree limbs, leaves, and even dead animals floating on top.

Now, a few yards to the left, the family spotted a farm wife in a sun bonnet on her knees working the dirt around her black-eyed Susans by the front gate to her yard.

Seeing this woman, all the travelers—as was their habit as they passed each house or met each wagon heading west—said

"Hello," and waved, to which the woman, getting up from the ground and brushing the dirt from her dress, said, "Stop right there! You'ns look like you've been pulled through a know hole backwards and then forwards again. I couldn't live with my conscience 'less you stop here and eat dinner with us!"

Immediately, Andrew thought the loss of time meant loss of miles and looked doubtful and perturbed.

But the lady, introducing herself as Rosanah Bogle, came right up to the wagon as it slowed down and took hold of the traces, indicating her earnestness.

Uncle Lee said to his brother-in-law, "We are the worse for wear, Andrew; let's take her up on her offer."

By this time, from inside the house and from the barn lot, people appeared: Rosanah's husband James; daughter Julia; son Otis; cousin Phebus, Grandma Chatburn; hired hand George; and Julius Caesar, their dog. After introductions and handshakes all around, James laughingly elaborated that Julius Caesar actually ruled the roost here, and "Look, he is taking to your children right off. That is a good sign as Julius is a great judge of character. Won't you stay, rest a while, and eat?"

Andrew's resolve to move on melted at this. "Yes, we'd be honored to be guests at your table," he said, smiling yet somewhat embarrassed. When it came to giving to people, Andrew was a natural, but accepting from strangers was a new, awkward, uncomfortable feeling to him. Mary, of course, picked up on this and said to him, in a lowered confidential voice, "It's OK, Andy, We'd do the same if this were turned around and we were the hosts." Andrew answered, "Yep, I guess we would all right."

So the guests unhitched their horses and then fed and watered them in the barn, at which point James asked, "Where are you heading?" to which Andrew served up an abbreviated story of how all this came to be and what their destination was.

Shutting the stall door on the two tired horses, James inquired as they left the barn, "How many miles is your trip going to be?"

"I studied the map before we left, and it looked like about 500 miles or so," Andrew answered.

"Glad it's you and not me," James laughed. "I am not a good traveler. I guess you'd say I'm a homebody that likes to stay put."

"I described myself just that very way until about a year ago. Now I hear opportunity knocking, and I'm going to open the door," Andrew responded.

In the kitchen, Rosanah had extended her table, adding four leaves to it, until it stretched from one wall to the other.

"In our old house, out back about a half a quarter," she said while setting the table with white Ironstone dishes, "we had in our kitchen no room at all, just space for a tiny table for four, but in this new house, the table can be made large enough for 12— 14 if you really squeeze, which we have had to do on occasion."

She went on to explain that she and James had been married 14 years ago and had lived in that small house out back with her parents, John and Eveline Chatburn. When the new house was about half done, her dad had died in a threshing accident, and so her mother had come to the new house to live permanently when it was finished.

"We just could NOT get along at all without Ma," Rosanah said affectionately, encircling her mother's waist and squeezing her.

The meal was quite a treat. Mary was especially grateful because the hands that prepared it were not her own. However, the food—including fresh pork and new potatoes, along with canned corn and blackberries—was heavenly.

As the meal ended, Andrew said, much out of character, "This is our eighteenth day on the road, and you fine folks are the only ones who have offered us more than a drink of water. We appreciate your kindness. We can't thank you enough."

"Won't you spend the afternoon and night with us? After a good night's sleep, you'll be ready to tackle the rest of your way," James urged.

"That is mighty tempting, but we plan to be camped on the east side of Union tonight, and time is a wasting," Andrew responded.

Mary hugged Rosanah and Grandma Chatburn, saying, "We'll never forget your generous hospitality." The men shook hands.

"Our best goes with you as you head on to Illinois," Rosanah said and waved as the wagon lurched into its slow movement again.

In Union, Mary bought a sack of coffee beans for 30 cents, remarking, "We'll make some coffee and eat the leftover biscuits and elderberry jelly Rosanah sent with us for supper. That ought to hold us till morning."

What an energizing, optimistic lift the Bogles had given them, a brief rest on a grueling journey.

May 2, 1890. Camped tonight by the side of the road about 2 miles from Union. Had better roads since we left there.

CHAPTER 19
Breakdown

"Bloom Hotel
Saturday, May 3, 1890
Dear Ma and Pa, Since we have been gone from home 19 days, I thought you might like to hear from us.

I am in Wildwood, Missouri, this afternoon, about 30 miles or so west of St. Louis, waiting on some repair work at the wheelright's.

This morning we were surprised to find the land much leveled off, compared to what we've traveled over since entering Missouri 12 days ago. The roads seem to improve the closer we get to St. Louis; more civilization is the cause, I suppose.

After going about three hours, I said to Lee (Mary's brother who joined us unexpectedly the same day we crossed the state line—a big help to us all, and so chipper), 'This road is much smoother than what we've been on, and because of fewer hills, now we can see better what's up ahead before we're smack right on it. I think we might speed up, don't you?' Lee said that was a good idea, so we coaxed the horses up a notch. We've had slow, slow progress many days so that this improved pace was welcome—each yard of ground behind us brings us closer to our destination, which we're weary to see.

At that clip, then, we moved on another hour or so till the sun was straight overhead.

Well, my suggestion was actually a bad one as it turned out. Unseen by us was a hold in the road covered by sticks and leaves, and at the bottom of which was a sharp boulder.

When the wagon hit this jagged rock, the front right wheel stood the impact fine, but when the back wheel, bearing most of the weight of our possessions, slammed down in that hole, Crack, two spokes of the wheel snapped like peach tree switches. This, in turn, allowed the felloe and the tire to bend inward to the space where the broken spokes created a weakness. This "out of round" wheel had to be fixed, of course, as you both understand from your own experience with wagons and buggies.

At any rate, we shored up the rear axle with stacked big rocks and took off the wheel, which I tied a rope to and dragged it on horseback to this town.

You'll notice I'm writing on hotel stationery. I came in here and paid 25 cents for paper, pen, and ink so I could write you while waiting for the wheelright. He said the repair would take a couple of hours—that he had to replace the two spokes with seasoned oak wood. The fellow is made, he said, from ash, and the iron tire must be hammered back to its original curve.

That's enough about our wheel. It should be back in service and we should be on our way by early evening, with a little daylight left. I guess we're lucky that we haven't broken down before now, considering the unbelievably hilly terrain and abundant mud. In some places, we have had to clear the road of fallen trees and furniture tossed out of wagons to lighten the load. A new wheel would have cost us around 25 dollars, which is more than my total budget saved up for the entire trip.

We're all in good health and doing as well as could be expected.

Ma, is your elbow better after that fall down the cellar steps? Pa, did that new calf ever take to taking nourishment? Have you heard from Uncle Bob and the girls in Idaho?

When you write us, mail it to Iuka, Illinois; that's the closest post office to us, as far as I know. It's a few miles west of our land; I will go there at least once a month and check.

Well, I've filled up five sheets of Bloom Hotel paper, front and back, with all this news.

Sincerely, your son, Andrew."

A side room in the hotel lobby served as the town's post office. Sealing up the envelope, Andrew stepped into this room and mailed the letter.

Back at the wagon, Andrew, Lee, and Mary secured the wheel on the axle lubricated with lard. Then they pushed up on the axle with all their strength while Charlie and Roy pushed and removed the top stone that supported it. Breathing a sigh of relief, the adults removed the remaining rocks, throwing them in the hole that had caused them all this trouble, delay, and expense.

Charlie and Andrew switched the horses and the wagon headed east once more. Mary, Roy, and Mabel sat in the wagon bed, and Uncle Lee rode behind on his horse humming and then whistling "Oh Susanah."

Having had lots of time to study the wagon during the breakdown, Charlie asked, "Pa, why are the front wheels of our wagon smaller than the back wheels?"

His dad, greatly relieved they were once again journeying on, explained, "Many years ago, son, as the covered wagon was developed to help people travel from one place to another with their possessions, people realized that smaller front wheels made it easier to turn the wagon. That's why."

Charlie took a long breath and felt contented; his dad knew the answer to everything.

The little band of travelers went along at a snail's pace, ever vigilant, now, of holes, limbs, rocks, and rock formations that were part of the road that might cause them further delay. The sun began to set behind them, casting the shadow of the covered wagon on the horses drawing it.

All of nature seemed to be alive this day. Wild cherry and dogwood trees were blooming, and non-blooming trees had nearly completely pushed out their year's green leaves.

A sense of hope and renewal was in the very air they breathed. Nature was on their side.

May 3, 1890. Camped tonight by the side of the road in a pleasant place about 23 miles west of St. Louis. Had good road today not very hilley. Quite pretty through here since we left Union.

CHAPTER 20
Haircuts

"Hold STILL, Roy—er, NO—there—you—moved—moved again, ROY!" Andrew, clearly out of patience, said. Taking a step back, scissors and comb in midair, he warned, "If you don't hold still, I cannot be responsible when I cut your ear off!"

When you're five years old, unconfined, accustomed to having complete freedom of movement any day and every day—except for church on Sunday—and free to try the limits of your growing limbs and muscles, the necessity of sitting motionless and being sheared like a sheep is almost impossible to take seriously. At least, that was true in Roy's case.

Roy dangled his feet in front of the wooden chair he was sitting in, his heels roughly colliding with the rungs that joined the chair legs.

"Please, PLEASE try to hold still for me. That means don't move your head in any way," Andrew urged, looking Roy straight in the face, eye to eye, thinking Roy would understand the seriousness of this and cooperate.

But as his dad stepped to the side to begin cutting again with Grandma Stevens' big, clumsy sewing shears, at that precise moment, Roy felt an itching in his left nostril which, involuntarily, he scratched and dug at with his thumb and forefinger. Oh, he thought, drawing his forefinger under his nose, back and forth like a violin bow, that ITCHES. Any adult could have cautioned him that if he didn't stop scratching his nose, it would be completely cut off, and he would nevertheless have continued to scratch it vigorously. Oh, and between his shirt collar and the back of his neck, in that trough, he felt hair attacking his neck like barbed wire. Little stickers—thorns!— were digging into his skin, irritating it beyond belief. And now HIS EARS!! How they itched! Hair must have flown in his ears! With his little fingers, he made drill-like motions, attempts to remove or dislodge the hair but only driving it deeper into the ear canal.

"Mary," Andrew said, rolling his eyes heavenward, "if they hadn't already looked like sheep dogs, with a hank of hair to constantly push away from their eyes, I would NEVER have attempted this." He stretched a lock of hair up and then horizontal over Roy's left ear.

ZING, the scissors' blades came together and sheared the shock of hair to about half its length. Roy's hair was dark and coarse. And, except for a few dousings in creeks, it had been unattended and unwashed for 20 days. The same was true for all the travelers. Limited water supplies were used only for cooking and drinking. Except for an occasional spit bath, they didn't—couldn't—bathe.

Not an experienced or confident barber, Andrew despised this hair cut day. In Falls and in Abilene, a barber had been paid to do this. However, under these circumstances of duress, he would have to do. Also, this was Sunday, and the kids should look respectful and at their best for church; in fact, they all should and would, even if it was, again, a makeshift service outside.

When, at least, Andrew called Roy's haircut finished and Roy sprang from the chair, shaking his neck and shoulders like a dog fresh out of a pond, it was Charlie's turn. Thankfully, for Andrew, this haircut was uneventful. Charlie held completely still throughout the entire procedure, even though Andrew didn't advise him to. Being two years older than Roy and possessing a more serious, less flighty nature, Charlie gave his dad no grief; the shears reduced his mop of hair by about half.

Mary then snipped a little hair from both Andrew and Lee. She was very uneasy about this and would only use the small scissors she used in cutting threads in tatting. Her own hair remained unshorn; she brushed it and yanked it back, forming a bun at the base of her neck.

Church began. They were all, in appearance, the best they could be that day in God's presence. Mary knew they looked pretty ragtag, and she silently asked God to forgive the disheveled way they looked.

All six people joined hands in a circle, and, just like it was the other two Sundays, Andrew prayed, thanking God for their safe passage this far, praising God for sending Jesus to redeem them from their sins, and asking God to continued to see them through to the end of their journey.

Using a tin plate with a piece of bread and a granite cup filled with water, Lee served communion, reminding them, symbolically, of the body and blood of Christ.

Mary led the singing with a repeat of "Amazing grace, how sweet the sound, that saved a wretch like me," followed by "Will the circle be unbroken, by and by, Lord, by and by? Is a better home awaiting in the sky, Lord, in the sky?"

These songs took Mary back to the church services of her childhood, contrasting so sharply with her family's service today. Yet, she remembered her pastor often quoted the scripture that said that where two or three are gathered in His name, God is there.

Among the many changes required by this trip—and other changes yet to be required at their new home in Illinois—Mary mused, would the future bring changes to their faith? Or was it more accurate to think that their faith would help them adapt to the changes required of them, and that it was their faith that would not change?

If six people have a religious service at the side of a mud road, then God is there. She comforted herself with this thought since worship in such a crude form was new and uncomfortable to her. She felt that adapting and meeting challenges head on were most definitely on their horizon.

May 4, 1890. Camped tonight in the timber. A nice place. Got water across the road where there is an empty log house. Came about 11 miles this afternoon. Are within 12 miles of St. Louis. The roads are nice. Andrew cut the boys' hair this forenoon.

CHAPTER 21
Across the River

"Pa, tell us more about the Elephant Test!" Charlie said to his dad.

Reading the road sign "Saint Louis—12 miles east" yesterday, the image of the Eads Bridge popped up in Andrew's mind.

As a math and science student at the Institute of Science in Topeka, 15 years ago, Andrew had, as part of his course of study, learned about the history and fundamentals of transportation and bridge construction, including Roman weight-bearing arches that figured in aqueducts and the Colosseum, and gothic windows, doorways, and vaulted ceilings of Renaissance cathedrals.

At the end of his first year at the Institute, 1874, the scientific world was all atwitter at a daring architectural project in St. Louis, Missouri: the Eads Bridge, spanning the 6,442 feet width of the Mississippi River. It was the longest arch bridge in the world; its use of ribbed steel and its use of steel as its basic structural material were controversial and caused many an argument and many a bet at the time.

Two of Andrew's teachers had diametrically opposing views about the construction of such a bridge. Professor Kingsbury said the bridge was the result of the brilliance of James B. Eads and would be a permanent monument to his greatness, while Professor Lundrenis swore to anyone who would listen that the first train over the bridge would cause its collapse and that ten million dollars would be instantly lost.

Previously, Andrew had given his children, Mary, and Lee all these details about the bridge so that when Charlie asked, again, about the Elephant Test, he just wanted his dad to repeat the entertaining story he'd heard already.

Therefore, Andrew began again, in midstream.

"So, to prove that the Eads Bridge was safe before its official opening to the public 16 years ago, John Robinson borrowed an elephant from a circus in town. With a large crowd of spectators on hand, Mr. Robinson and the elephant sauntered east on the bridge to Illinois, and the bridge stood firm. At the time it was thought that elephants had special senses that prevented them from stepping onto anything that might be hazardous to them. Also, Mr. Eads, the designer of the bridge, later had 14 locomotives go simultaneously back and forth on the bridge, and the bridge never shook."

Since Charlie and Roy had seen an elephant at a circus in Abilene the previous summer, they were amused at the thought of a man leading one across a new bridge. They could just see that in their mind's eye.

Roy asked, "Pa, is this the same bridge we are going over today in St. Louis?"

"Yes, that it is, Roy," his dad confirmed. "A drawing of the Eads bridge is right here in The Scientific American, an old magazine I used as a cushion between two plates in our old trunk. When I began thinking more about St. Louis the closer we got, I remembered this magazine and retrieved it."

"Will we be going up and down on those curved things of the bridge, Pa?" Charlie wondered.

"No, son," Andrew reassured him, "the two decks are level. The bottom road is for trains, and the top is for walkers, horseback riders, and horses and wagons."

This conversation took place at around 10 a. m. on the west edge of St. Louis as they ate; the meal was a combined breakfast and lunch of corn pones and bacon, both left over from the night before. Andrew had planned this day so that they would be into Illinois by noon, having heard that early morning and later afternoon were the most congested times on the bridge. And going through St. Louis at night was definitely out of the question for two reasons: St. Louis at night was unsafe, plus he wanted his family to see everything clearly as they went over the bridge.

Not knowing what to expect, commerce-wise, in Illinois, Andrew stopped the wagon a mile or so east of the St. Louis city limits to stock up at a general store that was quite on a higher level of prosperity and inventory than any they had seen in the last three weeks. There they bought, from the beautiful displays, ginger snaps for 20 cents, bread 25, prunes 25, lemons 10, tobacco 20, meat 30, hay 70, oats 50, sugar 25, bread 25, and corn 50.

And as they made their way through the busy streets and onto Market Street, they encountered a toll gate (10 cents) and a small toll bridge (20 cents).

Today was a major purchase day, with a total of $3.80 going out.

But Andrew did not begrudge the 35-cent Eads Bridge toll. Having never seen the structure, except in drawings, he grew more and more anxious as the wagon edged along the west bank of the Mississippi, the view of the river basically obliterated by huge multi-story warehouses and loading docks, passing the Catholic basilica with its spire standing our distinctly, heading north to where the bridge joined the land.

Giving way to horse and wagon and horse and buggy traffic that seemed to come at them from all directions and that seemed to have no rules or logic at all, Andrew, his hands firmly on the reins and his eyes making frequent arcs to avoid collision, made slow progress along the brick streets of the warehouse district. The sound of the horses' hooves on brick had a hollow effect to it, so different from the thud of hooves on dirt and the plop of hooves in mud.

Then, there it was: the bridge in its engineering and aesthetic magnificence. It did not disappoint them.

At the gate, Andrew handed over the required 35 cents for a horse-drawn wagon. Then he clicked the reins and the humble little band beheld the Mighty Mississippi and the bridge that the elephant tested.

Even at this hour, before noon, traffic was heavy, but there were more wagons heading west into St. Louis than going into East St. Louis.

While the eyes of Mary, Lee, Roy, Charlie, and Mabel swept from left to right—taking in the current of the river, the picturesque steam boats on the river and at the docks, the people and animals (lost of chickens in crates) on the wagons and on the horses they were meeting headed west, the small shacks that huddled right up against the muddy bank and the lapping water of the river—Andrew had less freedom to take it all in because he was concentrating on the horses. He had a fear that the horses would get nervous and maybe spooked being surrounded by other horses and wagons, both all around them and meeting them, too. Consequently, Andrew concentrated solely on his job of keeping his team calm and under control.

Luckily, the horses handled themselves well.

As they neared the Illinois side, Andrew said to his family, "Fix all of this scene in your minds. You might never see anything else in your life that equals it."

Turning their heads this way and that, they all made a mental image like a photograph.

The covered wagon rolled off the bridge and into a relatively opulent East St. Louis, with grand public buildings, wide streets, well-manicured lawns, spanking-new two- and three-story brick and stone homes. It all had the feeling of "new," as contrasted to the close, dirty, "old" atmosphere of St. Louis.

Consulting his hand-drawn map, Andrew announced that their next stop would be Belleville.

At the edge of East St. Louis, with a chill in the air, the paved brick road dropped off into dirt again, and Lee said, "So much for high living. We're back to the kind of roads we are oh so familiar with."

Clank, clank, the skillets and tools suspended from the hooks in the wagon beat a familiar cadence as the wagon headed up toward the big hill to the east.

Stopping the wagon abruptly, Andrew announced, "The horses are dead tired, and so are we. As soon as we tackle this big hill here and get a ways beyond it, we will call it a day."

Charlie added, "And tonight we'll all dream about bridges and elephants."

May 5, 1890. Camped about 5 miles East of Belleville. Came through St. Louis this forenoon and crossed the river. Roads very bad. It is cold today.

CHAPTER 22
Dreamers

Something was horribly wrong. And Charlie knew it.

He was, by himself, driving the wagon east over the Eads Bridge. The horses had started rearing and whinnying as he had never heard them do before.

Dusty winds blew horizontally across the bridge, and Charlie grabbed both the reins with his right hand, shielding his eyes with his left hand from the dry grit in the air.

The volume the hooves made on the plank decking of the bridge increased, then tripled so that it was as if Charlie's ear was pressed to all the planks at once, and the percussion of the hoof beats and the grinding of the wagon wheels drowned out all other sound. Charlie was still trying to control the horses, yet he could no longer hear their whinnying; he could only see their heads jerk up and down and side to side spasmodically.

Just then the dense cloud thinned out. Coming toward Charlie, head on, was an enormous white horse, bridled and saddled, but with no rider. It was at least one and a half times larger than Dock; its eyes were black and fierce, and it seemed steam came out of its enlarged nostrils.

Charlie thought, "I must stop the wagon and get that horse for its owner."

When the white horse was parallel to Charlie, he leaped from the wagon seat and succeeded in grabbing its pommel. His feet were swinging helplessly in the air and the horse galloped west toward St. Louis. He must get up in the saddle, turn him around, and catch up with his own wagon going the other direction. He could do it, he knew. He must.

· ·

Roy is the master of all he surveys, riding the Test Elephant on the Eads Bridge. At both ends of the bridge, thousands of well-wishers are cheering and waving handkerchiefs and flags.

Dressed in a red, black, purple, and gold ring master's suit, with matching top hand with an enormous gold feather tucked in its band, Roy lightly taps the side of the elephant with a silver switch. The elephant glides on, unaware of the switch, content and intent on its glorious duty of carrying Roy.

Roy smiles and broadly waves; the crowd on both ends roars it approval.

He tips his hat and bows his gracious gratitude.

Yes, he knew the elephant would not break the bridge. It hadn't shown the slightest weakness—no stress, no creaking, no yawning, no crumbling, no collapse. To the newspaper reporters, he had declared, before his trip across the bridge, "Just like the elephant who never forgets, may you always remember this afternoon, the day the Eads Bridge triumphantly held me and the Test Elephant."

Roy was a hero. He had saved the day. He continued his self-satisfied, delicious promenade across the bridge that spanned the Mississippi.

· ·

The monster was outside the window. She could hear it scratching the tree bark.

Raising her head and shoulders off the pillow and looking through the glass panes, she saw a black claw come toward the window as if it would smash through and grab her.

Mabel dropped back on her pillow, throwing the covers over her head.

In this position he stayed, paralyzed, for what seemed many minutes.

All was blackness and silence.

Curiosity, though, got the best of her, so she cautiously, just barely moving the corner of the blanket aside, peeped with her left eye to the window at her left.

A blood red eye, as big as a dinner plate, pressed against the window, staring directly at her with a knowing look that seemed to say, "You're not safe, you know. Not safe."

Mabel ran screaming out of the room to her mother downstairs, but her mother wasn't there. Mabel couldn't find her anywhere. Her parents' bed and all the furniture in their bedroom were gone. The lace curtains festooned inward, the wind coming through the open windows. Her mother had deserted her. Where was she? Where was she?

....

In the cow barn, Lee and his dad, Isaac, were throwing down hay into the manger below. The sun shone through the single window high over their heads in the gable.

Lee noticed that Isaac would not look him in the face like he usually did. And when Lee tried to gain eye contact with him, Isaac turned away and busied himself with the pitchfork.

Usually his dad joked around with him, no matter what the chore or situation. They were more than father and son; they were good friends.

Carrying a big tuft of hay on his pitchfork and throwing it down the V made the air hazy with dust. Then, Lee could sense that his father had stopped moving and avoiding him and was staring at him.

Slowly Lee discerned his father in a condition he had never before seen him in: he was crying.

In shock, speechless, Lee automatically looked away, trying to find words that he couldn't locate.

Time passed. Isaac said in a mournful, clear voice, "She's gone."

Lee's mind raced and he responded, "Mother—is—gone?"

"Yes, gone."

"You mean—dead?"

"No, she left me, she left us," Isaac muttered, shaking his head side to side in disbelief.

"But she needed us to take care of her. She can't care for herself or anybody else," Lee reasoned with his dad.

"I know, son, but she left late last night, with no explanation. She was the love of my life. Now she's gone," Isaac responded.

"You really loved her, Dad, in spite of the way she treated you—and us?" Lee questioned.

"She's gone. She's gone. She's never coming back," Isaac mourned.

The outside barn door squeaked as it opened. Peering down from the loft, Lee and Isaac could see Lee's mother standing inside the barn in her black traveling dress, her opaque eyes looking up at them in the loft and her right index finger beckoning them to come down to her.

....

Mary was high up in the air. All around her was brown water, below. The wagon lumbered slowly across the bridge.

Absolute and total fear of heights and of water was overwhelming her. Closing her eyes, hoping it would all go away didn't work, for when he looked around again, she was—again, as before—high above the muddy river.

This had to be the longest mile of her life.

Oh, but what was the wagon doing? It had turned and was now going west, instead of east.

Her stomach churned, and dizziness made objects and people fuzzy all around her.

The wagon was almost at the west end of the bridge ready for dry land when—it was going east again.

East, west, east, west the wagon went, each return trip terrifying her even more.

She clutched Mabel to her in the wagon bed, saying to herself, "We're never going to get off this bridge. Never—going to get off. Never going."

. . . .

Turning over in the cramped quarters of the wagon bed, Andrew abruptly sat up, loosened the back drawstring of the canvas top, and looked out at the ground.

A surreal scene it was. Positioned on the ground were some kind of circles.

Had someone drawn them with a big stick? Was this a prank Lee had done for a laugh?

Andrew rubbed his eyes and scooted out the back of the wagon. His feet, when they should have hit the ground, landed on something firm. Yes, he was standing on an object; not a rock, it was too regular in shape for that.

Bending down and touching the object he was standing on, he recognized it as the spoke of a wagon wheel. He followed the spoke out to the felloe and felt the cold iron outer tire.

Yes, it definitely was a wagon wheel, but it was on the ground, not on the wagon.

118

Stepping to the right and passing the corner of the wagon, he could see that the axle was bare. And continuing his walk around the wagon, he found each axle end had no wheels.

A wagon without wheels stood before him.

He must put the wheels back on.

He reached for the wheel he had stepped on, rolled it over to the axle, and tried to put it in place. Too small, the hole in the middle of the wheel was too small to go on the axle.

Returning to the back of the wagon, Andrew could see several—maybe dozens—of wheels laying on the ground that he hadn't noticed earlier.

Feverishly and sweating profusely suddenly, his heart beating wildly, he tried another wheel, no. Then another—too small. Another—way too big.

None of the wheels would work.

What could he do? He must fix this.

Try another—no, for a small cart. Another—no, for a much bigger wagon.

Over and over Andrew dragged wheel after wheel to the axle, none working. His thirst was excruciating. His head pounded with pain.

Now his anxiety reached panic. "I can do this. I can fix this. I can figure this out by myself," he said under his breath, all the while knowing that he could not do this and that it was hopeless.

How were they going to get moving again?

"Try another wheel. I have not tried them all. I know I can do this. Try another."

In the night, six people tossed and turned, dreaming their dreams.

May 6, 1890. Camped tonight in the timber under the hill. Stopped about 5 o'clock. Has rained all the afternoon. It is real cold. Cleared up this eve—Are in 3 or 4 miles of Frogtown. Terriable roads. So muddy. Andrew isn't feeling well.

CHAPTER 23
Handwork: The Apron

In her home back in Kansas, Mary's hands had not been idle for the past eight years. What with three babies in five years, she had literally had her hands full. And the first three years of her marriage, 1882-1885, had been consumed by, as people put it, setting up housekeeping.

Mary's days and evenings were filled to the bursting point with physical labor: starting a fire in the cook stove; carrying water from the cistern; making biscuits, bread, and pie crust dough; boiling, wringing out, and hanging out clothes to dry; ironing—oh, how she hated that—all the shirts, trousers, dresses, and underwear; darning socks, reattaching ripped pockets; and cutting out and sewing baby clothes and Andrew's shirts.

There was little or no time to do the handwork that Mary and her mother had bonded with during her adolescence. This time, about 1862-1882, was when Mary learned not only how to sew garments but also how to add character and flourishes through embroidery, appliqué, and tatting.

After a day's work was done, while her dad read a newspaper, book, or magazine, Mary and her mother would sit—basically in silence, except for the tick tock of the mantle clock and the rustling and folding of newspaper pages—and do work with needle and thread for hours on end. Luckily for them, the spinning wheel was becoming obsolescent, so that thread and cloth could be bought at a store, not made at home.

Mary's early marriage allowed little time for this handwork, and Mary missed it sorely. Her mother hand said that work with needle and thread was good training for the hands, discipline for the mind, and escape from worry. Mary had embraced the discipline part, but while occasionally sewing in the evenings by Andrew's side before the children, she nevertheless worried as her hands moved automatically with the sewing implements. Even though her mother had always said to "ease your mind by concentrating on the fluid up and under and in and out motion of the needle and thread," it never worked exactly that way for Mary, whose needlework was intricate and beautiful but whose worry was omnipresent. Was Andrew pleased with her cooking? Did she keep house according to his standards? Was she every going to have kids? Was her worrying so much worrying Andrew?

More worry was heaped on worry when she was pregnant with the children, giving birth, nursing, doctoring, and so forth, in the next five years, 1885-1890.

Charity Knapp, her mother-in-law, with all her bossiness and subtle manipulation of people to get her own way, often exasperated Mary, but Mary had to hand it to her mother-in-law when it came to handwork; she was an artiste.

And in early March of this year, Charity had suggested that she and Mary create for her a white apron, one bordered in manufactured lace, set together with a sewing machine, and appliquéd with scrolling leaves and flowers. Charity had helped her do all but the appliquéing, about which she said, "Mary, you can work on these designs during the idle moments of your trip."

Just as Charity's advice that Mary should go on this trip and that it would be good for her—as if bumping along 500 miles would benefit anyone's health—the idea that Mary could pull out embroidery during the journey to occupy her time was equally ridiculous. Cooking three meals a day on an open fire and looking after the children, alone, demanded most of her time and energy.

On this particular evening, now that the family was so near to its destination and since Mary had not taken one stitch on the apron along the way, Mary thought of it.

The days had gotten longer during their trip so that when the family had set up camp near Salem, finished supper, and had an hour of good daylight left, Mary went to her old trunk that held her most precious possessions—including her jewelry box with Mother of Pearl on the lid, the Knapp family pictures in two pieces, her chipped ironstone platter, and her mother's quilts made of tiny squares from her dresses of childhood—and pulled out the apron she and Charity had started, wrapped in an old sheet pinned shut.

Whew! It looked so tiny around—the band was exactly 20 inches, which was an ideal waist size for women of her day. It was just barely possible for band to encircle her waist and meet at her spinal column. Another baby or two and that would be all over, she thought.

Mary remembered her mother-in-law had drawn the design on the cotton cloth free hand with a pencil that she was to embroider and appliqué, including special French knots for more of an third dimension effect. She stood looking it, holding it up to the evening sun.

Would such a fussy apron have any place at all in the wilderness they were headed to? Would she perhaps need to put this apron away for a time in the future when they were established and could return to the style of living they had been born into? Would the apron torment her, reminding her of what they had left behind and couldn't retrieve?

Mabel switched up to her mother, and Mary, on a whim, tied the apron strings under Mabel's chin in a bow, letting the semi-oval shape of the lace and cotton form a sort of lacey bonnet for her in back.

"That's Ma's apron," Mary called out after her as Mabel danced and turned around the fire's embers.

"Mabel looks like a Pilgrim child," Charlie said, then repeating it in a sing-song pattern that Mabel adjusted her dance rhythm to, keeping time with Charlie's words as he sang them gleefully.

Lee sidled up to Mary, observing, "That child's wearing an apron for a hat. I've been thinking that that may be what we will all have to do in our new location: adapt to the new, using the old in unfamiliar ways. Agree, Andrew?"

Spitting a big wad of amber tobacco juice at the base of a pokeberry bush, Andrew said, "That may well be just the approach of thinking we need, Lee."

Before Mabel ripped the apron on branches of the wild dewberry bushes that carpeted the roadside, Mary pulled it off of her head from the front and folded it, thinking, "No work on this tonight after all, but after we get our start, I'll finish it."

May 7, 1890. Camped tonight within 2 miles of Salem on the side of a clay hill. Has been a little warmer today. Roads better.

CHAPTER 24
The Marquis

Every minute was now bringing the Knapps closer to the reality of what their lives would become.

Never having seen their destination, the anticipation of seeing it had increased in intensity as their odyssey progressed these last few days. Their new home was like a Christmas package, all wrapped in finery in their heads and they were all ready to open it to see what was inside. The vague notion of a new location was becoming a more focused picture.

Andrew pictured the 120 acres as Marquis L. Burns, the previous owner, had described it to him: beautiful, lush, green, and like the Garden of Eden where he, like Adam, would tend it. Other biblical references came to his mind in regard to his land, all positively idyllic: the land of milk and honey, living off the fat of the land, marching to Zion, the Promised Land. These images and the emotions they privately stirred deep in him gave him such a supreme state of well-being that could only be termed joy. This land symbolized peace, serenity, independence, self-reliance, success, and family stability. True, he had had his doubtful moments during the last six months, but now that this trip would soon conclude and he would cross over the Jordan, he was seized with a mental inebriation. It would be wonderful, everything he dreamed it would be, he was sure. Inwardly, he rejoiced.

Mary, on the other hand, was a great deal more conflicted about this new home in Illinois. A blend of her father's optimism and her mother's pessimism, Mary's mind vacillated about it all. She had promised Roy—and herself—on their departure, that she was done with crying about leaving Kansas, that she would uproot and establish a new life in Illinois for the good of her family, putting her gut feelings aside and not complaining or regretting the change. While she had kept the tears at bay these 24 days on the road, her mind—in conscious thought and in dreams—had been a ship of mutinous activity: one minute she would straighten up and tell herself that this move was sensible and that there was nothing to be afraid of, yet another minute would usher in torrents of doubt and negativity, telling her that this was all tomfoolishness and loss. She thought, what a game your mind could make of a new challenge; within one psyche, two opponents could be grappling with each other in a wrestling match, each opponent savoring a moment's advantage and then being overpowered by the adversary, neither every claiming a decisive victory, the struggle continuing.

Lee's attitude about the unseen land was much less disturbed, for he was literally along for the ride. He might stay at their destination, or he might not, depending on what they found and how it all worked out. "I'll just wait and see what happens," he said to himself, smiling.

The children, of course, had romanticized expectations about their new home, having been pumped up with hope by their parents. The foundation of their hope was as strong as a spider's web. Andrew and Mary wanted their kids to be happy—even though they had left behind the only home and family they had ever known—so an appealing vision of their new home in Illinois had been cultured in them, like the heated gas that causes a multi-colored hot air balloon to rise in the sky.

Driving through Iuka, Andrew asked a general store proprietor, "Can you tell me how to get to the Burns land in Romine Township?" to which the man, Caleb Stinnett, answered, "Oh, you mean the Marquis? That's what we call him around here, although we've never met him. People say he lives way off down in Arkansas and just owns this land. Kind of a mysterious character—a name without a face. Actually Mr. Burns' name on the tax roll is officially 'Marquis Lucianus Burns.' Why do you ask where his land is?"

"I've bought it," Andrew answered, grinning at the sound of the man's complete name. Marquis Lucianus Burns—that sounded like a French land baron with Roman ancestry. "My family and I have come 500 miles from the Abilene, Kansas, area and we want to know how to get there, how to get to our new home."

"You keep going east on this road, which after a while will wind to the southeast. When you see the railroad tracks, right before them, turn south and go about a mile and a half, then turn back east. That will bring you to the Burns land. I'm the tax assessor for that land and I know it well," Mr. Stinnett explained. "But, may I ask, how did you come to buy 120 acres sight unseen? I say that since you don't have any idea where it is."

"The Marquis and I met on a train in Kansas. I swapped him my steam iron patent for his land," Andrew returned.

"You mean like an iron for pressing clothes?"

"That's what I mean, yes. I designed it, patented it, and he traded his land for it."

Rubbing his chin in confusion, Mr. Stinnett responded, "Well, I know nothing about the value of your steam iron idea, but I do know your land value. I'm just throwing around in my head the question of who got the better deal."

"I couldn't even hazard a guess at that," Andrew said, with a slight frown.

"The Marquis has been a land owner here for a few years, but he's never been here as far as we know. I've supposed the land was an investment of his. The only contact we've had with his is through the mailing of his tax debt and his mailing the amount back to the courthouse in Salem, always on time, check always good," Mr. Stinnett went on.

"That investment is ours now, and we're real anxious to get there and claim it. We paid our real estate taxes today in Salem," Andrew continued, trying to end the conversation.

"I don't see how you're going to live out there. Not even a well there, as I recall," Mr. Stinnett remarked.

Andrew affirmed, "We're determined to make a life out there. We'll make a go of it." The clicked the reins and they headed east.

When the wagon was out of the town, Roy asked his dad, "Who is this Mark Key you were talking about?"

Amused, Andrew said, "The Marquis is the reason we're out here this very minute trying to find our home, Roy. No, actually, he's the man I bought the land from with my steam iron patent."

"How much did it cost, Pa?" Charlie piped up.

"Son, that's our business only. I'm glad you didn't ask that question back in Iuka. If you promise never to tell anyone outside the family, I'll tell you the amount," Andrew said.

"I promise, Pa," Charlie said in earnest.

"For the 120 acres we're trying to find today, I gave him what we agreed was the value of my steam iron patent: 820 dollars. That's about seven dollars an acre. The Marquis," Andrew chucked, "was actually Marquis Lucianus Burns. He told me this land had a lot of centuries-old trees on it that I could mill land make a lot of money from. We'll see."

The actual sale of the land had taken place the year before on December 6, 1889, between the grantor—M. L. Burns and his wife Julia H. Burns, of Benton County, Arkansas— and the grantee—Andrew Knapp and his wife Mary E. Knapp, of Dickinson County, Kansas—and recorded in the old handwritten book of deeds in the Marion County Courthouse in Salem, Illinois. The location of the land was in Section 14, three-fourths of the north east fourth in three 40-acre parcels.

Between December 6, 1889, and April 15, 1890, huge, everlasting changes, like a strong chemical action, were at work in the immediate and extended Knapp families, culminating in these 24 days of travel.

Turning south before the railroad tracks, as Mr. Stinnett had instructed, the family came alongside an old woman, her long black dress hem swishing at the dampened road dust from the afternoon's rain. She was carrying a shallow, lidded basket, which Mary thought likely contained eggs.

"We're looking," Andrew said courteously, "for what was the Burns land that is now our own."

"What is called the Burns land—that used to be called the Stonecipher land—is about a half mile on south and then a quarter mile east from here. There are no fences to mark that land, so I don't know how you're going to know your own land even if you're standing in the middle of it," the old woman said in a sour tone, pointing south with an arthritic index finger.

Andrew responded respectfully, "Thank you, ma'm," and drove on.

Night was falling on this important day when the wagon rolled into the area according to the old woman's directions.

Andrew felt like Moses in the wilderness. The old woman had been right; there were no markers, no fences.

Darkness prevented going any farther toward their land of promise, so once again they set up camp among some trees, whose trees—his own or someone else's—he had no idea.

May 8, 1890. Tonight finds us camped on the Burns land not far from our own. Came through Iuka. Payed the taxes in Salem. Come through there this morning. Has rained some today.

CHAPTER 25

Promised Land

An owl hoo-hooted, seemingly answered by the high-pitched yipping of a coyote, in the early morning hours.

Andrew crawled out from under the wagon, wrapped in a worn quilt that Mary had said could mingle with the slightly damp ground with no harm coming to it.

The air was cold, very cold, for May, and he shivered.

Our new home in Illinois.

This is it, somewhere out there, he thought.

The sun hadn't risen, yet that faint glow was in the east, heralding its arrival.

In this semi-darkness, Andrew went to the back of the wagon. There lay a woman and three children, the most important human beings in his life. Had he come here, dragging them with him, for his own selfish motives? Or did he put them before himself, wishing for them a better life, a new start, independent of his family in Kansas? Or was it both? Or neither? Was he deluding himself?

An hour or so later, the sun was rising somewhere on their new home in Illinois.

Suddenly, he had to find it.

Reaching under the wagon with his foot, he prodded Lee awake, saying, "I can't wait any longer. Let's hitch up and set out for our land."

Mary, hearing voices, stuck her head through the drawstring opening and whispered, "Is something wrong? Andrew, are you all right?"

"Mary," Andrew whispered back, "I have got to see this thing we've blindly tied our lives to, this land, this 120 acres, I must see it. I can't wait, not another hour."

Try as they might to be quiet, the adults couldn't still the clanging of the old blackened pots and tools hanging from the hooks screwed into the hoops when the wagon headed east.

Awakened this way, the kids were disoriented and a little frightened.

"Ma, why are we moving in the dark?" Charlie asked, his blue eyes full of concern.

Pulling Roy and Mabel to her, Mary said, "Your pa is anxious—wants to see the land, our new home, immediately. Everything is all right. The sun is rising on a new chapter in our lives."

Mabel put her arms around her mother's neck, resting her head on her shoulder. In spite of the movements and noise of the wagon, soon her breathing changed and she was back asleep.

Roy sat, tee-pee fashion, a blanket covering him, half awake.

Charlie poked his head out the front drawstring and said to his dad and Lee on the wagon seat, "Will you recognize our home when we get there, Pa?"

"That's what we're going to find out," Lee answered, noting Andrew's dreamy, thinking state.

The horses plodded on east as they had done each day for the last 24. This day, to them, was not extraordinary. They snorted, lifting their heads in an affirmative up and down nod, and pulled on.

A well-fed raccoon lumbered along the dirt road. Last autumn's leaves and the winter's sticks and limbs obliterated the road bed; the wagon wheels crunched over the limbs, making a dry sound like someone cracking hickory nuts.

A rabbit, closely pursued by another, zinged across the road, barely missing the horses' hooves. They almost collided with a rotting limb speckled with mold and tiny mushroom-like circles of rubbery growth but, avoiding it, the pair leaped over and disappeared in the undergrowth of bushes and saplings as if a ready-made tunnel was waiting for them.

Sunlight couldn't shine directly on the east-bound travelers since tall trees on both sides of the road prevented it; plus, a T way down at the end of the road showed the same dense tree growth running north and south.

Almost at the T, Andrew stopped the horses. On his left, half grown over with vines and small trees, was a ramshackle-looking old house that looked, at best, to have been constructed in a few days, decades ago, to meet an urgent, temporary need. Now, in its abandoned state, two of four porch posts were rotted, allowing the west part of the overhanging roof to sag down. A screen door hung askew on its upper hinge only. Two front windows had broken panes of glass. A chimney sticking through the tin roofing was sloping to the north and looked in danger of toppling over with the next strong wind.

This, of course, could not be their new home, Andrew surmised, so he looked straight ahead along the north-south road wondering it that was the direction of their new home.

Uncle Lee jumped down from the wagon bed and, with hands on hips, took in the scene. After some time, he reacted, saying, "Andrew, Mary," to which Mary popped her head out the front drawstring, "I think we need a guide, someone to identify the land you bought. With no fence, or marker of any sort, we strangers just can't do it."

After a pause, Andrew agreed, saying, "And that person is Caleb Stinnett back in Iuka. A tax assessor could help us lay claim to what is ours. That crotchety old woman in the black dress got us out this far, and I feel we are probably in the right general area, but how can we find the exact 40, 40, and 40 acres? You know, I told you that the land is 40 acres to the north, 40 acres to the south of that, and 40 acres to the east of that. It's like it makes an L shape." Gazing at the huge old trees before him, Andrew said, "Lee, would you mind to go for Mr. Stinnett? I'll stay with Mary and the children. Now that we're finally here, I feel I need to keep my eye on what is mine, or what I think is my own land—*as if someone could come along and take it away from me,*" he said ironically.

"Let me get old Thunder saddled, and we'll be gone. He's been just a tagalong horse for many days. Hope he hasn't forgotten how to gallop," Lee laughed.

"Hurry back, Lee," Mary said as he trotted off west.

· · — · · — · · — · · — · · — · · — · · — · · — · · — · · — · · — · · — · ·

"Mr. Stinnett, my sister's family and I passed through here yesterday on our way to find their new home. And, although we followed your directions with a bit of help from a cranky old lady along the road, we can't be sure that we've actually found it. Could you maybe ride over there with me and identify the land and its boundaries?" Lee respectfully requested of the store owner back in Iuka.

Walking to a side door, Mr. Stinnett called, "Edna, Ednaaaa, Edna Stinnett, could you come in here?"

A perky little woman with almost white hair and calico bonnet came through the door, half running.

"I told you and I told you that you could NOT measure and cut that muslin without ..." but she stopped, seeing Lee instead of a seamstress as she expected. "Er, I mean, I, oh, Caleb, you have me so frustrated now I can't even talk. What's the matter?" she asked, drying her hands on her apron.

"This is Mr. Stevens, Edna," Caleb said, somewhat embarrassed by his wife's brusqueness. "We talked about the Knapp family he's with who bought the Burns 120. Could you handle the store without me for a few hours while I help these people claim their land?"

"Land's sake, Caleb, is that all?" she replied in a lyrical voice with the "all" uplifted in tone. "You just go along out there. Wasn't I running this store before I married you, anyway?" she elaborated, pinching his cheek impishly and doing a little mincing step.

Removing his apron and throwing it in a chair behind the cash register, Caleb picked up his plat book, saying, "We'll need this to authenticate it all. As soon as I get my horse around back, we'll be on our way."

. . . .

When Lee and Caleb were within a quarter mile of the wagon, they observed all five Knapps in a row, studying the trees to the east.

Lee and Caleb dismounted and tied their horses to the wagon.

Caleb, shaking Andrew's hand and tipping his hat to Mary, said, "You can give your horses a long rest now, Mr. Knapp. This is, indeed, your land. Your journey is over."

An enormous relief coursed through Andrew's veins.

Getting his plat book from his saddle bag, Caleb turned to Section 14, Romine Township, Marion County, Illinois, 1887.

"Are you positive we're in the right place? I won't squat on someone else's land," Andrew asked.

"Right here," Caleb said, pointing to the Section 14 part of the map, "are the three forties you own. Three years ago when the book was printed they belonged to M. L. Burns, see," he explained. "Now they are yours."

With great interest, Andrew said, "Yes, that's the man, Marquis L. Burns, and that's the configuration of it I had in my head from talking to him about it when we swapped patent for land—an L jutting to the east just like the drawing shows. Can you show us around, so to speak, Mr. Stinnett?"

It felt good to be walking, not riding, on the road. The land started about an eighth of a mile south of where the wagon had stopped. At the exact point where their 40 started, Mr. Stinnett searched for and found in the thick undergrowth a survey monument, made of concrete and topped with a brass cap.

Mr. Stinnett, gesturing to the engraving on the brass a series of letters and numbers, said, "The Federal Government, in 1880, had the land in many states surveyed so that land could be homesteaded. Surveyors laid out sections, townships, and ranges so that ownership and location would not be later disputed. These monuments—or markers—were set in place, and the surveying could continue from that point in any direction, with the surveyor's plumb going exactly over the cap of the marker. Let's walk on up the road now. After about 440 adult steps, or 1320 baby steps—both of which equal a quarter of a mile—we'll stop and look for another marker." Mr. Stinnett located the second marker. Up another quarter mile was the end of the west side of their land.

"Most of this 120 is virgin timber, Mr. Knapp, except for a small area around the house," Mr. Stinnett remarked.

"House? Where is it?" Andrew spoke anxiously. "Mr. Burns said it was average size, one-story. That's all I know about it."

"As I recall, Mr. Knapp," Mr. Stinnett went on, scratching his head, "it's not too far from here, around to the east, in the corner of this 40."

Walking east rapidly, Andrew inquired, "A lot of these trees have had damage, big sections ripped off like broken toothpicks. Have you had any ice storms in recent years?"

"No, no ice storms, but we had a big twister through the county last month. People lost some of their buildings. A neighbor of mind had to shoot his milk cow because a picket from his fence was driven right through the rib cage—in one side and out the other—by the twister. And, you know, when they butchered that cow, they found the picket was still whole and unsplintered, not broken up as you might expect it to be. Imagine the force of such a thing," Mr. Stinnett said, shaking his head in disbelief.

Roy, looking up at his mother, said, "Ma, I'm hungry, and I'm thirsty. We haven't had anything to eat or drink all day."

"In all this excitement," Mary said, "we've been distracted, but we'll go back to the wagon and soon start dinner."

A few more yards brought them to a lane, which Mr. Stinnett turned into, the rest of them following, pushing small trees aside, stomping saplings and vines underfoot, ducking under branches extending from large trees.

To make it easier to keep up, Mary picked Mabel up while Roy walked immediately in her shadow to benefit from all she cleared out of the way. Mabel clung to her mother's neck like a cat, shutting her eyes to the leaves and snapping twigs that her mother made her way through.

Up ahead, Mary heard Andrew say in an awful, tragic tone, "Oh, my God!" She could only see the feet and legs of Charlie, Andrew and Mr. Stinnett as she bent down under a broken-off branch, the top of which rested in the V of an adjacent tree. She worked to release her skirts snagged by a wild rose bush that encircled and then ran up this host tree. Hearing Andrew saying, "I don't believe it! It can't be!" she stopped her patient work and just yanked on her dress, leaving at least a yard of it in the rose bush. When Mary tugged on her dress, Mabel shifted, swinging free, just holding her neck. As all of Mabel's weight was supported by her neck, pain shot through her neck, spine, and shoulders. White lights appeared in front of her eyes. Struggling the remaining few feet, with her head down to dodge more limbs and to minimize the pain, she finally saw Andrew's feet directly in front of her and lifted her head up.

Roy was at her side and Mabel opened her eyes. They all stared at what was once... a house.

Seven people looked at it with speechless amazement.

The roof rested against three giant oak trees. It had been peeled back from the house—like an open trunk lid wrenched from its hinges. The entire west half of the house looked as if a mammoth buzz saw had started at the foundation and had worked its way in a diagonal direction, leaving 2 by 6's with upright ends that resembled immense match sticks snapped in two, the jagged edges looking like the back of a porcupine.

To the east, one room remained relatively unscathed, the wooden bed frame with its corn husk mattress and grimy patchwork quilt smoothed as if it had just been made.

Rain and snow had wrecked all that was exposed, leaving mildew and swollen, distorted, and warped wood in its wake.

"The tornado. Must have been last month's tornado," Mr. Stinnett lamented.

Charlie, the practical thinker, questioned, "Pa, what are we going to do now. Where are we going to live?"

Unsuccessfully, Mary tried to shush him, but he continued, "We've come 500 miles, and now we don't even have a house!"

Andrew—weary, downtrodden, nauseated, hungry, thirsty, saddened—put his left hand on Charlie's right shoulder, searching for words that wouldn't express the enormous ache in his heart and soul, finally, after some moments, in a peaceful, controlled, serene voice, responded, "You know, there are worse things, son, than losing a house. Just consider this. What if we had begun our move on March 15, instead of on April 15? Think about that, son."

Charlie pondered the full magnitude of the question, but while he thought about it, Roy broke in, "We'd all be dead today, probably."

That fact made electricity shoot through Mary's spine and the muscles of her arms and legs. It was true, she knew; a month earlier and that would all have been dead, except for maybe if one of them had been in the back bedroom, and that person would have immediately become a widow, a widower, or ... an orphan.

Taking a big gulp of air and making a sigh with it, Mr. Stinnett, surveying all the destruction around them, said, "Can I show you the rest of your place?"

The family turned around with the same spirit and facial expressions people have when they leave a graveyard: behind them was an undeniable, unpreventable loss, and they would have to go on with their lives, nevertheless.

Mr. Stinnett guided the heavy-hearted people around their boundaries, first ¼ mile east, then ¼ mile south, ¼ mile east, ¼ mile south, and finally ½ mile west, back to their starting place at the first survey monument.

Looking back to the northwest at the shanty they had remarked on and thought uninhabitable earlier in the day, Andrew questioned Mr. Stinnett, "Who owns the land with that falling-down house on it?"

Consulting the plat book, he answered, "That belongs to James Jones, who moved a few years ago to Idaho to try his luck. If you're a mind to, I think it would be permissible for you all to live there for as long as you need to."

Andrew sighed, seeing all his family's eyes fixed on him, and said, "I don't see that we have any other choice today. But that doesn't mean that will be true next month, six months from now, or next year. We've got a lot of work and planning to do first, but that house will do for today."

Caleb Stinnett shook hands with Andrew, Lee, and Mary and tugged at the ear lobes of the kids, who shrank back, giggling. "I'll be seeing you in my store?" he questioned.

"You can count on that, Mr. Stinnett," Andrew responded. "Thank you."

And off Mr. Stinnett rode, taking one glance over his shoulder at the homeless people behind him, thinking of the hardships they were facing and would face.

"Lee, let's get our axe and shovel and clear the way into that hovel over there. Charlie, you can pull the wagon into this north-south road, back it up, and pull it up into the driveway of that house. Mary, would you and Roy search for some water? You may have to walk back to the creek he went through, Skillet Fork, Mr. Stinnett called it; what a curious name for a creek. After Lee and I clear our way to the porch, we'll cut a small tree, using the trunk of it to prop up the sagging roof. By nightfall, we'll have smoke coming out of that old chimney and a roof—such as it is—over our heads."

Confidence and optimism abounded in Andrew and radiated to Mary, Lee, and the children, all of whom set to work, under his leadership, doing their appointed tasks. Mabel played in the wagon with three rocks and a stick she had picked up on their excursion: with the stick as a magic wand, the rocks morphed into three beautiful ladies and then later into three dogs, in her play of make believe.

But Andrew was not playing make believe. He was a realist who now clearly saw the job that was his: to tame this wilderness he had claimed, to ultimately establish a saw mill that would bring an income from the eons-old trees all around him. But first, there were the practical matters at hand. He and Lee chopped and dug. Charlie managed to get the wagon in place, although the backing was a difficulty. Mary and Roy each carried a bucket of water from the Skillet Fork, Roy sloshing about half of his bucket full on the ground along the way as the bucket banged against his leg.

The porch supported and secure, Lee and Andrew blazed a trail inside, finding an old fireplace from which they shoveled debris; they gathered big sticks of wood, sawing them and starting a fire. This fireplace had a hook so that Mary could suspend her iron pot from it, without using the tripod.

By dark, a pot of white beans seasoned with a chunk of cured ham bubbled in the fireplace, and the family ate, sitting on the freshly-swept floor, this simple meal with a few crackers each sitting on the freshly-swept floor. Suddenly, they could hear a gentle rain pinging on the metal roof, such a different sound than rain made on the wagon's canvas cover.

Although the house looked better than it had in the morning hours, Mary and the children balked at sleeping on the damp, rough, uneven floors; in one of the smaller rooms, a cherry-bark oak tree was growing through a hole in the floor. Beds would come later when they had improved the floors, Mary said, "And when we remove the indoor forest."

After a day of tromping around and eating only one meal, the kids didn't have to be coaxed to go to sleep. All three lay down in the wagon bed and were asleep about as fast as it takes to blow out a kerosene lamp.

Friday, May 9, 1890. A full moon illuminated the woods to the east. Andrew, Mary, and Lee stood with their backs against the wagon bed in the drive of this dilapidated old house and pondered the woods.

Andrew had noted various trees on their tour today: maples, pin oaks, burr oaks, sycamores, cedars, black walnuts, and hackberries. These sturdy trees pushed their limbs heavenward like inverted feather dusters. Below them were shorter trees: white dogwoods in bloom, redbuds, persimmons, and wild cherries, under which were poke bushes and sumacs. Honeysuckle, poison ivy, wild grape, poison oak, and trumpet vines scrambled up these bushes and up into the trees. Thistle, Queen Anne's lace, black-eyed Susans, and blue bells made a pretty, lasting picture in Andrew's mind; they painted his land with vibrant color.

"This place is wild and beautiful, and it's our task to harness it and make it work for us," Andrew said.

"And we can do it, Andy," Lee encouraged.

"Mary, what's your opinion of it all?" Andrew asked her, stealing his arm about her waist.

"I think this is quite a change in life for us. We have no decent home, no church to worship in, no close water supply, no nearby family or friends, no garden spot worked up and planted, and no way in the world to harvest all that timber you're staring at," she observed.

Andrew's heart was in his throat. She didn't like it. Why would she?

"I take it, Mary," Andrew started, "that you're not happy about this and that —."

In his midsentence, she stopped him, saying, "You're wrong, Andrew. I don't see this as hopeless. I'm not unhappy. I see this as a challenge and a test for us. A minister back in Nora Springs when I was a teenager said that all of life is a test, the score of which determines your place in eternity. That thought comes to me, facing our future here. Our future is here; our future is what we make of this place. I firmly believe 'All things work together for good to them that love God, to them who are called according to his purpose.' Our purpose is in this place."

Andrew kissed Mary lightly on the cheek, Lee modesty averting his eyes.

A light rain began to fall.

The three concentrated on the flickering shadows the moon and a light west wind made on their promised land.

May 9, 1890. Tonight finds us in a shanty just across the road from our own land. Got dinner in a fire place. This is quite a change in life for us. It is raining this evening.

Manufactured By: RR Donnelley
Breinigsville, PA USA
January, 2011